Oh, no. Now she recognized that shifty look for what it was.

Her parents had just found her yet another suitable man to date. They'd invited him to dinner, so then he'd feel obliged to ask Victoria out to dinner.

Maybe she really was tired, or maybe she'd gone temporarily insane, because she found herself saying, "Well, it'll be nice for him to meet my fiancé."

"Fiancé?" Diana stared at her in shock. "You're engaged?"

Oh, no. Saying she was dating would've been enough. She really shouldn't have panicked and made up an engagement, of all things, but when she opened her mouth to backtrack, the lie decided to make itself that little bit more tangled. "Yes, I know it's ridiculously fast, but you know when you meet The One, don't you, Mom?" She gave Samuel a sidelong glance.

"You mean, you and Samuel?" Patrick asked, his jaw dropping.

"Yes." She took Samuel's hand and squeezed it, sending him a silent plea to run with this for now and she'd explain and fix things later.

Dear Reader,

I love visiting country houses, and somehow I managed to talk my editor into a country house book where my hero and heroine are complete opposites *and* have a fake engagement :) Victoria, my heroine, is a little bit too serious and earnest (mind you, she has a lot to be serious about), whereas Sam, my hero, is a bit too laid-back.

As they work on fund-raising events to save Victoria's ballroom, they find themselves falling in love with each other. But when their fake engagement takes on a life-threatening spin, will they find their happy-ever-after?

I thoroughly enjoyed the research for the book—not just the desk research about costume and recipes (and there might have been some tinkering in my kitchen) but actually visiting country houses. Special thanks to the team at Blickling Hall for answering my questions—any errors in the book are my own—and to my husband, Gerard, and dear friend Jo for coming on the visits with me.

With love,

Kate Hardy

A Diamond
in the Snow

—

Kate Hardy

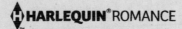
HARLEQUIN®ROMANCE

Recycling programs
for this product may
not exist in your area.

ISBN-13: 978-1-335-13533-9

A Diamond in the Snow

First North American publication 2018

Printed in U.S.A.

Kate Hardy has always loved books and could read before she went to school. She discovered Harlequin books when she was twelve and decided this was what she wanted to do. When she isn't writing, Kate enjoys reading, cinema, ballroom dancing and the gym. You can contact her via her website, katehardy.com.

Books by Kate Hardy

Harlequin Romance

Summer at Villa Rosa

The Runaway Bride and the Billionaire

Falling for the Secret Millionaire
Her Festive Doorstep Baby
His Shy Cinderella
Christmas Bride for the Boss
Reunited at the Altar

Harlequin Medical Romance

Miracles at Muswell Hill Hospital

Christmas with Her Daredevil Doc
Their Pregnancy Gift

Paddington Children's Hospital

Mommy, Nurse...Duchess?

Unlocking the Italian Doc's Heart
Carrying the Single Dad's Baby

Visit the Author Profile page
at Harlequin.com for more titles.

For Jo Rendell-Dodd, with love and thanks
for coming on my research trip, and Megan,
with love and thanks for putting up with a
recalcitrant author! xxx

Praise for
Kate Hardy

"I was hooked...*Her Festive Doorstep Baby* is a
heart-tugging emotional romance."

—*Goodreads*

CHAPTER ONE

'VICTORIA?' FELICITY, THE textile conservation expert who was doing the annual survey of the displays at Chiverton Hall, stood awkwardly in the office doorway. 'Could I have a quick word?'

Victoria's heart sank. Felicity and her team were checking for anything that might need conservation work over the winter. The fact that she wanted a word must mean she'd found something. 'Bad news?'

'It's not *all* bad,' Felicity said brightly. 'There are a couple of rooms where you need to lower the light levels a bit more, to limit the fade damage, but those moth traps have worked brilliantly and there's no evidence of silverfish or death watch beetle—all the holes in the wood are the same as they were last time round and there's no evidence of frazz.'

Frazz, Victoria knew, were the little shavings of wood caused by beetles chomping through it.

And that would've meant major structural repairs to whatever was affected, anything from a chair to floorboards to oak panelling. 'I'm glad to hear that.' Though she knew Felicity wouldn't have come to talk about something minor. 'But?'

Felicity sighed. 'I was checking the gilt on a mirror and I found mould behind it.'

'Mould?' Victoria looked at her in shock. 'But we keep an eye on the humidity levels and we've installed conservation heating.' The type that switched on according to the relative humidity in a room, not the temperature. 'How can we have mould?' A nasty thought struck her. 'Oh, no. Is there a leak somewhere that's caused dampness in a wall?' Though Victoria walked through the rooms every day. Surely she should've spotted any signs of water damage?

Felicity shook her head. 'I think it probably started before you put in the heating, when the humidity wasn't quite right, and we didn't spot it at the last survey because it was behind the mirror and it's only just grown out to the edge. Unless we're doing a full clean of the wall coverings—' something that they only did every five years '—we don't take the mirrors and paintings down.'

'Sorry.' Victoria bit her lip. 'I didn't mean it to sound as if I was having a go at you.'

'I know. It's the sort of news that'd upset anyone.'

Victoria smiled, relieved that the conservation expert hadn't taken offence. 'Which room?'

'The ballroom.'

Victoria's favourite room in the house; she loved the way the silk damask wall hangings literally glowed in the light. As children, she and Lizzie had imagined Regency balls taking place there; they'd dressed up and pretended to be one of their ancestors. Well, Lizzie's ancestors, really, as Victoria was adopted; though Patrick and Diana Hamilton had never treated her as if she were anything other than their biological and much-loved daughter.

'I guess behind the mirror is the obvious place for mould to start,' Victoria said. 'We don't use the fireplaces, so there's cold, damp air in the chimney breast, and the dampness would be trapped between the wall and the mirror.'

'Exactly that,' Felicity said. 'You know, if you ever get bored running this place, I'd be more than happy to poach you as a senior member of my team.'

Victoria summoned a smile, though she felt like bawling her eyes out. Mould wasn't good in any building, but it was especially problematic when it came to heritage buildings. 'Thanks, but I'm never going to get bored here.' Though if Lizzie, the true heir to Chiverton Hall, had lived, she would've been the one taking over from their parents. Victoria probably would've ended up working in either food history or conservation but with books, rather than with textiles. 'How bad is it?'

'Bad enough that we'll need to take the hangings down to dry them out. We can't fix it in situ. Hopefully a thorough clean with the conservation vac and a soft brush will get out most of the damage, but if the material's been weakened too much we'll have to put a backing on it.'

'Worst-case?' Victoria asked.

'The silk will be too fragile to go back, and we'll need a specialist weaving company to produce a reproduction for us.'

Victoria dragged in a breath. 'The whole room?'

'Hopefully we can get away with one wall,' Felicity said.

Even one wall would be costly and time-consuming. 'I know the actual cost and time to fix it will depend on what the damage looks like on the reverse side, and the wall might need work as well,' Victoria said. 'I'm not going to hold you to an exact figure but, just so I can get a handle on this, can you give me a ballpark figure for the worst-case scenario?'

Felicity named a figure that made Victoria

wince. It was way over the sum she'd allocated for maintenance in the annual budget. And she knew the insurance wouldn't cover it because mould counted as a gradually operating cause. She'd have to find the money for the restoration from somewhere. But where?

'Short of a lottery win or me marrying a millionaire—' which absolutely wasn't going to happen because, apart from the fact she didn't actually know any millionaires, she wasn't even dating anyone, and her exes had made it very clear that she wasn't desirable enough for marriage '—I'm going to have to work out how to fund this.'

'Start with heritage grants,' Felicity advised. 'You'll have a better case if you can show that whatever you're doing will help with education.'

'Like we did when we installed the conservation heating—putting up information boards for the visitors and a blog on the website giving regular updates, with photographs as well as text,' Victoria said promptly.

'And, if we pick the team carefully, we can have students learning conservation skills under our supervision,' Felicity said. 'The ballroom is a perfect example of a Regency interior, so it's important enough to merit conservation.'

Victoria lifted her chin. 'Right. I'd better face the damage.'

Felicity patted her shoulder. 'I know, love. I could've cried when I saw it, and it's not even mine.'

It wasn't really Victoria's, either. Even though her father had sorted out the entail years ago, so the house would pass to her rather than to some distant male relative, she wasn't a Hamilton by birth. Her parents loved her dearly, just as she loved them; but she was still very aware that their real daughter lay in the churchyard next door. And right now Victoria felt as if she'd let them all down. She was supposed to be taking care of her parents and the house, for Lizzie's sake, and she'd failed.

Actually seeing the damage made it feel worse.

Without the mirror over the mantelpiece to reflect light back from the windows opposite, the room seemed darker and smaller. And when Felicity turned off the overhead light and shone her UV torch on the wall, the mould growth glowed luminescent.

'The hangings from that whole wall are going to have to come down,' Felicity said. 'With polythene sheeting over it, to stop the spores spreading.'

'And everyone needs to be wearing protective equipment while they do it,' Victoria said. 'And we'll have to measure the mould spores in the air. If it's bad, then we'll have to keep visitors out of the room completely.'

Felicity patted her shoulder. 'Don't worry. We'll get this fixed so the ballroom shines again.'

Victoria was prepared to do whatever it took. Fill out endless forms, beg every institution going for a loan. Or find a millionaire and talk him into marrying her and saving the ballroom. After her ex had been so forthcoming about where she fell short, Victoria was under no illusions that she was attractive enough for an ordinary man, let alone a millionaire who could have his pick of women; but she knew from past experience that the house was a real draw for potential suitors. All she needed was a millionaire instead of a gold-digger to fall in love with it. Which kind of made her a gold-digger, but she'd live with that. She'd be the perfect wife, for the house's sake.

When Felicity and her team had left for the day, Victoria walked up and down the Long Gallery with her dog at her heels, just as countless Hamilton women had done over the centuries, not seeing the ancient oil paintings or the view over the formal knot gardens. All she could think about was what a mess she'd made. She wasn't a coward—she'd tell her parents the news today—but she wasn't going to tell them until she'd worked out a solution.

Pacing cleared her head enough for her to spend half an hour on the Internet, checking things. And finally she went to her parents' apartment.

'Hello, darling. You're late tonight. Are you eating with us? I've made chicken cacciatore—your favourite,' her mother said.

'You might not want to feed me when you hear the news,' Victoria said with a sigh. She wasn't sure she was up to eating, either. She still felt too sick. 'Felicity found a problem.'

'Bad?' Patrick Hamilton asked.

She nodded. 'Mould in the ballroom, behind the mirror. They found it when they were checking the gilt. Best-case scenario, they'll take the hangings down on that wall, dry them out, remove the mould and put backing on the weak areas of silk. Worst-case, we'll have to get reproduction hangings made for that whole wall. We won't know until the hangings come down.' She dragged in a breath. 'Hopefully we can get a heritage grant. If they turn us down because they've already allocated the funds for the year, then we'll have to raise the money ourselves. We'll have to raise a bit of it in any case.' And she had ideas about that. It'd be a lot of work, but she didn't mind.

'Firstly,' Patrick said, 'you can stop beating yourself up, darling.'

'But I should ha—' she began.

'It was behind the mirror, you said, so nobody would've known it was there until it reached the edge,' Patrick pointed out gently. 'If I'd still been running the house, the mould would still have been there.' He narrowed his eyes at her. 'You're too hard on yourself, Victoria. You're doing a brilliant job. This year has been our best ever for visitor numbers, and your mother and I are incredibly proud of you.' She could hear the worry and the warmth in her father's voice and she knew he meant what he said. But why couldn't she let herself believe it? Why couldn't she feel as if she was *enough*? 'Lizzie would be proud of you, too,' Patrick continued.

At the mention of her little sister, Victoria's throat felt thick and her eyes prickled with tears.

'It'll work out, darling,' Diana said, enveloping her in a hug. 'These things always do.'

'I've been thinking about how we can raise the money. I know we usually close from half-term so we have a chance to do the conservation work before the visitor season starts again, but maybe we could open the house at Christmas this year. Just some of the rooms,' Victoria said. 'We could trim them up for Christmas as it would've been in Regency times, and hold workshops teaching people how to make Christmas wreaths and stained-glass ornaments and old-fashioned confectionery. And we could hold a proper Regency ball, with everyone in Regency dress and supper served exactly as it would've been two hundred years ago.'

'Just like you and Lizzie used to pretend, when you were little and you'd just discovered Jane Austen.' Diana ruffled her hair. 'That's a splendid idea. But it'll be a lot of extra work, darling.'

'I don't mind.' It wasn't a job to her: she loved what she did. It was her *life*.

'We can hire in some help to support you,' Patrick said.

Victoria shook her head. 'We can't afford it, Dad. The cost of fixing the ballroom is going to be astronomical.'

'Then we can try and find a volunteer to help you,' Patrick said.

'Yes—I can ask around,' Diana added. 'There's bound to be someone we know whose son or daughter is taking a gap year and would leap at the chance to get experience like this. We could offer bed and board here, if that would help.'

'Maybe this could be the start of a new Chiverton tradition,' Patrick said. 'The annual Christmas ball. In years to come, your grandchildren will still be talking about how you saved the ballroom.'

Grandchildren.

Victoria knew how much her parents wanted grandchildren—and she knew she was letting them down there, too.

The problem was, she'd never met the man who made her want to get married, much less have children. Her relationships had all fizzled out—mainly when she'd discovered that the men she'd dated hadn't wanted her, they'd wanted the house and the lifestyle they thought went with it. Once they'd discovered the lifestyle didn't match their dreams, she hadn't seen them for dust. And she'd been stupid enough to be fooled three times, now. Never again.

She'd fallen back on the excuse of being too busy to date, which meant her parents had taken to inviting eligible men over for dinner. Every couple of weeks they'd surprise her with someone who'd just dropped in to say hello. It drove her crazy; but how could she complain when she was so hopeless and couldn't seem to find someone for herself?

Maybe the one good thing about the ballroom restoration was that it might distract her parents from matchmaking. Just for a little while.

'A new tradition sounds lovely,' she said, and forced herself to smile.

'That's my girl,' Patrick said, and patted her on the shoulder. 'We'll find you some help. And we'll get that mould sorted. Together.'

Sam felt a twinge of guilt as he parked on the gravel outside his parents' house. He really ought to come home more often. It wasn't that far from London to Cambridge, and he was their only child. He really ought to make more of an effort.

His first inkling that something might be wrong was when he walked into the house with a large bouquet of flowers for his mother and a bottle of wine for his father, and his mother started crying.

He put everything he was carrying onto the kitchen table and hugged her. 'If I'd known you were allergic to lilies, Mum, I would've brought you chocolate instead.'

'It's not that. I love the flowers.' She sniffed.

He narrowed his eyes. 'What, then?' Please, not the unthinkable. Several of his friends had recently discovered that their parents were splitting up and were having a hard time dealing with it. But his parents' marriage was rock-solid, he was sure.

'It's your dad. He had a TIA on Wednesday night—a mini-stroke.'

'*What?*' Wednesday was three days ago. He

stared at her in horror. 'Mum, why on earth didn't you call me? I would've come straight to the hospital. You know that.'

She didn't meet his eye. 'You're busy at work, sweetie.'

'Dad's more important than work, and so are you.' He blew out a breath. 'Is he still in hospital? Is he all right? And how are *you* doing?'

'He's recuperating at home, and I'm fine.'

The first bit might be true, but the second definitely wasn't. 'Mum, I hate that you went through this on your own.' On Wednesday night, he'd been out partying. Without a clue that his father was in the emergency department with a potentially life-changing illness. 'What did the doctors say?'

'That if he wants to avoid having another one, or even a full-blown stroke, he needs to take it easier. Maybe think about retiring.'

Which was Sam's cue to come back to Cambridge and take over Patrick's place as the head of the family firm of stockbrokers. Leave the fast-paced, high-octane job he loved in the buzzing, vibrant capital for a staid, quiet job in an equally staid, quiet city.

He pushed the thought aside. Of course he'd do the right thing by his family. He wasn't *that* shallow and selfish, whatever his girlfriends liked to claim. There was a good reason why he kept all his relationships light. He'd learned the hard way that women saw him as a golden ticket to their future. Which wasn't what he wanted.

'And he needs to cut down on alcohol, stop smoking the cigars he thinks I don't know about, eat more healthily and take more exercise,' Denise added.

Sam glanced at the wine: his father's favourite. 'So this was the worst thing I could've brought him.'

'It's not your fault, love.'

'So, what—porridge rather than bacon for breakfast, no salt, and no butter on his vegetables?' Which meant his father wasn't going to be happy.

Denise nodded. 'But they've given him medication to thin his blood and stop another clot forming.' She bit her lip. 'Next time, it might be a full-blown stroke.'

Which might affect his father's speech, his mobility and his ability to think clearly. Sam's duty was very clear. 'I'll call my boss tonight and hand in my notice. I'm coming home to support you.'

'We can't ask you to do that, Sammy.'

'You're not asking. I'm offering,' he pointed out, and hugged her again. 'Mum, I want you to promise me you'll never deal with anything like this on your own again. You call me. It doesn't matter what time of day or night. You and Dad come first.'

She blinked away tears. 'Oh, Sammy. I know you've got a busy life in London. I didn't want to bother you.'

'It bothers me a lot more that you didn't tell me,' he said grimly. 'Promise me.'

'I promise,' she said.

'Good. Put the wine in the rack, and I'll think of something else to give Dad. Where is he?'

'In the living room. He's, um, not in the best of moods.'

Sam could imagine. 'I'll get him smiling, Mum.'

Alan Weatherby was sitting in an armchair with a rug over his knees and a scowl on his face.

'Hey, Dad.' Sam patted his father's shoulder. 'On a scale of one to ten of boredom, you're at eleven, right?'

'Your mother fusses and won't let me do anything. She says I have to rest.'

But his father wasn't known for sitting still. Resting would be incredibly frustrating for him. 'Maybe we could go to the golf club and shoot a couple of holes,' Sam suggested.

Alan rolled his eyes. 'It's play, not shoot. Which just shows you're a complete rookie and you'll hack divots out of the green and embarrass me.'

Sam didn't take offence. He knew how he'd feel in his father's shoes: cooped up, miserable and at odds with the world. 'A walk, then,' he suggested. 'I could take you both to the university botanical gardens.' A place he knew his mother loved. 'And we could have a cup of tea in the café.' Though without the scones and clotted cream he knew his father would like. 'A change of scenery might help.'

'Hmm,' Alan said.

'In your shoes, I'd be bored and grumpy, too,' Sam said. 'But your health's important, Dad. You need to look after yourself, especially as you're—'

'I'm not old, before you say it,' Alan cut in. 'Sixty-three isn't old. There's plenty of life in me yet.'

'And I want it to stay that way,' Sam said. 'The medics told you to take things easier, eat well, take a bit of exercise and reduce your stress.'

'Your mother's trying to make me eat lentils. *Lentils.*' Alan looked disgusted.

Sam couldn't hide a grin. 'They're not as bad as you think.'

'Don't *you* start. I thought you'd bring me contraband.'

He had. But only because he hadn't known the situation. 'No chance. I want you about for a lot longer.'

'Is that why you're dragging your feet about settling down and having children?'

If only his father knew. But Sam hadn't told any of his family why he'd broken his engagement to Olivia, two years before. Or why he'd got engaged to her in the first place. Even now it left a nasty taste in his mouth. Nowadays he made sure his girlfriends knew that he was looking for fun and not for for ever. Olivia had broken his ability to trust, and he wasn't sure he wanted to take another risk with his heart.

'No,' he said. 'Dad, there's an easy solution to all this.'

Alan frowned. 'What?'

'Let me take over Weatherby's from you,' Sam said. 'You've more than earned some time off to play golf and have weekends away with Mum. And I've spent the last six years in the City, learning the ropes. You'll be leaving the business in safe hands.'

Alan shook his head. 'The fund you manage is high risk. It's extreme. Half of our clients would look at your record, panic, and find themselves another stockbroker.'

'Apart from the fact that any strategy I recommended to a client would depend on the client's attitude towards risk,' Sam said dryly, 'I'm good at my job, Dad. That's why they promoted me.'

'You take risks,' Alan repeated.

'Calculated ones.'

'You're still young and reckless.'

'I'm twenty-seven,' Sam said, 'and I'm not reckless.'

'Prove it.'

Sam frowned. 'How?'

'Take an ordinary job for three months.'

'How's that going to prove anything?' Sam asked, mystified.

'It'll show me that you can connect to people in the real word. That you can see that actions have consequences.'

'Dad, I already do connect to people in the real world, and of course I know that actions have consequences,' Sam said, frowning.

'Take an ordinary job,' Alan repeated. 'Show me that you can take directions and listen to other people.'

Which had absolutely nothing to do with running a firm of stockbrokers, Sam thought.

Either he'd accidentally spoken aloud, or his doubts showed on his face, because Alan said softly, 'It's got everything to do with running the firm. It's about listening and relating to people—staff as well as clients. In London, you live in a bubble. You're insulated from your investors and everyone you mix with is like you—young, well-off and living in the fast lane.'

Most people would consider that Samuel Weatherby had made a success of his career. He'd got a job on his own merits after university rather than expecting to be a shoo-in at his father's business, he'd shown an aptitude for fund management and he'd been promoted quickly. But it sounded as if his father thought his job was worthless, and that hurt.

'Not all,' he said. 'There's Jude.' His best friend was an actor with a growing reputation on the stage, and people were talking about him in terms of being the Olivier of his generation.

'Right now,' Alan said, 'I don't think you're settled enough to work at Weatherby's. If I let you take over from me now, it'd be more stressful than running it myself.'

Sam reminded himself that his father had had a rough week—a mini-stroke that had brought him face to face with the idea of getting old or even dying, the prospect of having to change all the things he liked most about his lifestyle and feeling stuck at home when he wanted to be doing what he always did. Right now, Alan was simply lashing out at the nearest target—his son.

'Take an ordinary job for three months, and

if you can do that then I'll be happy that I'm leaving the family business in safe hands,' Alan said.

Sam could tell his father to forget it and stomp off back to London in a huff. But the fear he'd seen in his mother's eyes stopped him. Alan was at risk of another mini-stroke or even a full-blown one. Sam couldn't stand by and watch his father drive himself into an early grave. 'So what sort of job do you have in mind, Dad?' he asked.

'Actually, now you mention it, there is one,' Alan said. 'Working for one of my clients. Nice chap. He owns a stately home. A building problem's cropped up in the last week or so and they need to raise some money. He was talking to me about cashing in some investments, but as the market's just dipped I think now's not a good time.'

Raising money. Sam was very, very good at turning small funds into big ones. But he had a feeling that this particular client wouldn't be comfortable with the high-risk strategy he'd need to adopt to do that.

'The job would be voluntary,' Alan continued, 'because they can't afford to pay anyone. You'd be helping to organise the fundraising events.'

Sam couldn't help smiling.

'What's so funny?' Alan demanded.

'You wanted me to get an ordinary job. I thought you meant something in retail or a call centre. Ordinary people don't own stately homes, Dad.'

'No,' Alan said crisply, 'but their visitors and staff are ordinary and you'll be interacting with them.'

'A voluntary job.' Three months with no salary. But he'd be on garden leave; and even if that didn't work out, he'd managed his personal investments well enough that he could easily afford to take a sabbatical. Jude was coming back from a tour in rep to a three-month run in the West End and could stay at Sam's flat; it would save Jude having to find a landlady who was happy to have a theatrical lodger, and in return Sam would know that his flat was in safe hands. 'OK. I'll talk to him and see if I'll be a good fit.'

'Good.' Alan paused. 'The botanical gardens and afternoon tea, you said.'

'One scone, no cream, and no sugar in your tea,' Sam said.

Alan rolled his eyes. 'You're as bossy as your mother.'

Sam grinned. 'More like I'm as bossy as you, Dad.'

'You might have a point,' Alan allowed. 'Go and tell your mother to get ready. I'll have a word with Patrick and see if we can line up a chat for tomorrow.'

And Sam would have a quiet chat with his boss. This was time for payback. He wasn't thrilled with the idea of working in a stately home for three months, but if that was what it took to make sure his father stayed healthy and happy, he'd do it.

CHAPTER TWO

'So what do you actually know about this man who wants to come and help us, Dad?' Victoria asked.

'He's my stockbroker's son,' Patrick said.

'So is he taking a gap year? Is his degree going to be in history?'

'I don't know,' Patrick said, 'but Alan said he's very keen.'

He must be, Victoria thought, to arrange an interview for nine o'clock on a Sunday morning. 'Did you want to interview him, then, as you know his father?'

Patrick smiled and patted her shoulder. 'Absolutely not, darling. You're the one he's going to be working with. It needs to be your decision.'

'If you change your mind, we'll be in the office,' Victoria said.

It was a shame her father had been so vague about the details; he hadn't even asked for a rudimentary CV. Then again, her father came from the era of the gentleman's agreement and he didn't like paperwork. Hopefully the lad would bring his exam certificates with him and she'd be able to get an idea of his education so far and his interests, and whether he'd be the right one to help her.

Part of her thought there was something rude and arrogant about interviewing a volunteer for a job you weren't actually paying them to do; on the other hand, if he was hopeless, he'd be more of a hindrance than a help because she'd have to double-check everything he did. Plus, even though he wasn't being paid, he was getting valuable experience that might help him with applications for further study or a job in the heritage sector.

'Come on, Humphrey,' she said to her fox-red Labrador, who was curled up on the chair where he knew he wasn't supposed to be. 'Let's go for a walk.' It was more to clear her head before the interview than anything else. It felt as if she'd spent weeks wrestling with forms.

At the W-word, the Labrador sprang off the chair, wagged his tail and followed her into the garden.

Growing up at Chiverton had been such a privilege. Victoria loved everything about the place, from the mellow golden stone it was built from, through to the big sash windows that surrounded the huge Venetian window at the back of the house, through to the pedimented portico at the front. She loved the gardens that sprawled around the house and were full of daffodils and bluebells in the spring, the way the sunrise was reflected in the lake, and the formal knot garden at the side full of box and lavender. And most of all she loved the ballroom.

Her plans were going to require a lot of organisational skills. But hopefully Samuel Weatherby would fall in love with the place, too, and support her fundraising effort.

Humphrey headed straight for the lake as soon as they were outside and was already swimming after the ducks before she had a chance to call him back.

'I'm banishing you to the kitchen,' she said when he finally came out of the lake and shook the water from his coat. 'I don't want you scaring off our volunteer.' Unless he was unsuitable—and then perhaps she could offer him a coffee in the kitchen, and Humphrey would leap all over their volunteer and make him withdraw his offer of help.

She could imagine Lizzie's soft giggle and, 'But, Tori, that's so *naughty*!' Lizzie was one of the two people Victoria had ever allowed to shorten her name.

She shook herself. She didn't have time for

sentiment right now. She needed to be business-like and sort out her questions for her impending visitor to make sure he had the qualities she needed. Someone efficient and calm, who could use his initiative, drive a hard bargain, and not mind mucking in and getting his hands dirty. And definitely not someone clumsy.

In return, he'd get experience on his CV. She tried not to feel guilty about the lack of a salary. So many internships nowadays were unpaid. Besides, as her mother had suggested, they could offer him accommodation and meals; and Victoria could always buy him some books for his course. Textbooks cost an arm and a leg.

She changed into her business suit and had just finished dealing with an email when the landline in her office shrilled. She picked up the phone. 'Victoria Hamilton.'

'May I speak to Mr Hamilton, please? It's Samuel Weatherby. I believe he's expecting me.'

He sounded confident, which was probably a good thing. 'Actually,' she said, 'you're seeing me. I'm his daughter and I run the house.' She wasn't going to give him a hard time about asking for the wrong person. The message had probably become garbled between their fathers.

'My apologies, Ms Hamilton,' he said.

He was quick to recover, at any rate, she

thought. 'I assume, as you're ringing me, you're at the gate?'

'Yes. I parked in the visitor car park. Is that OK, or do I need to move my car?'

'It's fine. I'll come and let you in,' she said.

Humphrey whined at the door as she walked past.

'You are not coming with me and jumping all over our poor student,' Victoria told him, but her tone was soft. 'I'll take you for another run later.'

The house was gorgeous, Samuel thought as he walked down the gravelled drive. The equal of any London townhouse, with those huge windows and perfect proportions. The house was clearly well cared for; there was no evidence of it being some mouldering pile with broken windows and damaged stonework, and what he could see of the gardens was neat and tidy.

He paused to read the visitor information board. So the Hamilton family had lived here for two hundred and fifty years. From the woodcut on the board, the place had barely changed in that time—at least, on the outside. Obviously running water, electricity and some form of heating had been installed.

Despite the fact that the house was in the middle of nowhere and he was used to living and working in the centre of London, a few minutes away from everything, there was something about the place that drew him. He could definitely work here for three months, if it would help keep his father happy and healthy.

All he had to do was to convince Patrick Hamilton that he was the man for the job. It would've been helpful if his father had given him a bit more information about what the job actually entailed, so he could've crafted a CV to suit. As it was, he'd have to make do with his current CV—and hope that Patrick didn't look too closely at it or panic about the hedge fund management stuff.

He glanced at his watch. Five minutes early. He could either kick his heels out here, on the wrong side of a locked gate, or he could get this thing started.

He took his phone from his pocket. Despite this place being in the middle of nowhere, it had a decent signal, to his relief. He called the number his father had given him.

'Victoria Hamilton,' a crisp voice said.

Patrick's wife or daughter, Sam presumed. He couldn't quite gauge her age from her voice. 'May I speak to Mr Hamilton, please? It's Samuel Weatherby. I believe he's expecting me.'

'Actually,' she corrected, 'you're seeing me. I'm his daughter and I run the house.'

Something his father had definitely neglected to tell him. Alarm bells rang in Sam's head. Please don't let this be some elaborate ruse on his father's part to fix him up with someone he considered a suitable partner. Sam didn't *want* a partner. He was quite happy with his life just the way it was, thank you.

Then again, brooding over your own mortality probably meant you didn't pay as much attention to detail as usual. And Sam wanted this job. He'd give his father the benefit of the doubt. 'My apologies, Ms Hamilton.'

'I assume, as you're ringing me, you're at the gate?'

'Yes. I parked in the visitor car park. Is that OK, or do I need to move my car?'

'It's fine. I'll come and let you in,' she said.

He ended the call, and a couple of minutes later a woman came walking round the corner.

She was wearing a well-cut dark business suit and low-heeled shoes. Her dark hair was woven into a severe French pleat, and she wore the bare minimum of make-up. Sam couldn't quite sum her up: she dressed like a woman in her forties, but her skin was unlined enough for her to be around his own age.

'Sorry to keep you waiting, Mr Weatherby.' She tapped a code into the keypad, opened the gate and held out her hand to shake his.

Formal, too. OK. He'd let himself be guided by her.

Her handshake was completely businesslike, firm enough to warn him that she wasn't a push-over and yet she wasn't trying to prove that she was physically as strong as a man.

'Welcome to Chiverton Hall, Mr Weatherby.'

'Sam,' he said. Though he noticed that she didn't ask him to call her by her own first name.

'I'm afraid my father hasn't told me much about you, other than that you're interested in a voluntary job here for the next three months— so I assume that either you're a mature student, or you're changing career and you're looking for some experience to help with that.'

She thought he was a student? Then again, he'd been expecting to deal with her father. There had definitely been some crossed wires. 'I'm changing career,' he said. Which was true: just not the whole truth.

'Did you bring your CV with you?'

'No.' Which had been stupid of him. 'But I can access it on my phone and email it over to you.'

'Thank you. That would be useful.' Her smile was kind, and made it clear she thought he wasn't up to the job.

This was ridiculous. Why should he have to

prove himself to a woman he'd never met before, for a temporary *and* voluntary post?

Though, according to his father, they needed help. Having someone clueless who'd need to take up lots of her time for training was the last thing she needed. In her shoes, he'd be the same—wanting someone capable.

'Let me show you round the house,' she said, 'and you can tell me what you want to get out of a three-month placement.'

Proof for his father that he could take direction and deal with ordinary people. If he told her that, she'd run a mile. And he needed to get this job, so he could stay here to keep an eye on his parents. 'Experience,' he said instead.

'Of conservation work or management?'

'Possibly both.' He felt ridiculously underprepared. He'd expected a casual chat with a friend of his father's, and an immediate offer to start work there the next week. What an arrogant idiot he was. Maybe his father had a point. To give himself thinking time, he asked, 'What does the job actually entail?'

She blew out a breath. 'Background: we do an annual survey to check on the condition of our textiles and see what work we need to do over the winter.'

He assumed this was standard practice in the heritage sector.

'My surveyor found mould in the silk hangings in the ballroom. It's going to cost a lot to fix, so we're applying for heritage grants and we're also running some fundraising events.'

'So where do I come in?' he asked.

'That depends on your skill set.'

Good answer. Victoria Hamilton was definitely one of the sharper tools in the box.

'If you're good at website design, I need to update our website with information about the ballroom restoration and its progress. If you're good at figures, then budgeting and cost control would be a help. If you've managed events, then I'd want you to help to set up the programme and run them.'

Help to, he noticed. She clearly had no intention of giving up control. 'Who fills the gaps?' he asked.

'Me.'

'That's quite a wide range of skills.'

She shrugged. 'I started helping with the house as soon as I was old enough. And Dad's gradually been passing his responsibilities to me. I've been in charge of running the house for two years. You have to be adaptable so you can meet any challenge life throws up. In the heritage sector, every day is different.'

Her father believed in her, whereas his didn't

trust him. Part of him envied her. But that wasn't why he was here.

'I'll give you the short version of the house tour,' she said.

Stately homes had never really been Sam's thing. He remembered being taken to them when he was young, but he'd been bored and restless until it was time to run around in the parkland or, even better, a children's play area. But he needed to look enthusiastic right now, if he was to stand any chance of getting this job. 'I'd love to see around,' he fibbed.

She led him round to the front. 'The entrance hall is the first room people would see when they visited, so it needed to look impressive.'

Hence the chandelier, the stunning black and white marble floor, the artwork and the huge curving double staircase. He could imagine women walking down the staircase, with the trains of their dresses sweeping down behind them; and he made a mental note to ask Victoria whether any of her events involved people in period dress—because that *was* something he could help with, through Jude.

There were plenty of portraits on the walls; he assumed most of them were of Hamilton ancestors.

'Once they'd been impressed by the entrance hall—and obviously they'd focus on the plasterwork on the ceiling, not the chandelier—visitors would go up the staircase and into the salon,' she said.

Again, the room was lavishly decorated, with rich carpets and gilt-framed paintings.

'If you were close to the family, you'd go into the withdrawing room,' she said.

Another sumptuous room.

'Closer still, and you'd be invited to the bedroom.'

He couldn't help raising his eyebrows at her.

She didn't even crack a smile, just earnestly explained to him, 'They didn't just dress and sleep here. A lot of business was conducted in the private rooms.'

'Uh-huh.' It was all about money, not sex, then.

'And if you were really, really close, you'd be invited into the closet. This one was remodelled as a dressing room in the mid-eighteen-hundreds, but originally it was the closet.' She indicated a small, plain room.

He managed to stop himself making a witty remark about closets. Mainly because he didn't think she'd find it funny. Victoria Hamilton was the most serious and earnest woman he'd ever met. 'Surely the more important your guest, the posher the room you'd use?'

'No. The public rooms meant everyone could

hear what you were talking about. Nowadays it'd be the equivalent of, say, video-calling your bank manager about your overdraft on speaker-phone in the middle of a crowded coffee shop. The more privacy you wanted, the smaller the room and the smaller the number of people who could overhear you and gossip. Even the servants couldn't overhear things in the closet.'

'Got you. So that's where you'd plot your business deals?'

'Or revolutions, or marriage-brokering.'

He followed her back to the salon.

'Then we have the Long Gallery—it runs the whole length of the house. When it was too cold and wet to walk in the gardens, they'd walk here. Mainly just promenading up and down, looking at the pictures or through the windows at the garden. It's a good place to think.'

She flushed slightly then, and Sam realised she'd accidentally told him something personal. When Victoria Hamilton needed to think, she paced. Here.

'Next door, in the ballroom, they'd hold musical soirées. Sometimes it was a piano recital, sometimes there would be singing, and sometimes they'd have a string quartet for a ball.'

'The room where you have the mould problem,' he remembered. Was she blinking away tears? Crying over a *room*?

'We've tested the air and it's safe for visitors—you don't need a mask or anything,' she said.

He wasn't going to pretend he knew much about mould, other than the black stuff that had crept across the ceiling of his friends' houses during his student days. So he simply followed her through.

'Oh.' It wasn't quite what he'd expected. The walls, curtains and upholstery were all cream and duck-egg-blue; there was a thick rug in the centre of the room, a grand piano, and chairs and chaises-longue laid out along the walls. There were mirrors on all the walls, reflecting the light from the windows and the chandelier.

'It's not a huge ballroom,' she said. 'Big enough for about fifty, and they'd have supper downstairs in the dining room or they'd lay out a standing supper in the Long Gallery.'

'Is it ever used as a ballroom now?' he asked, intrigued.

'Not for years, but I'm planning to use it as part of the fundraising. It'll be a Christmas ball, with everyone wearing Regency dress, and dinner will be a proper Regency ball supper.'

Her dark eyes were bright, and it was the first time Sam had seen her really animated. It shocked him to realise how gorgeous she was, when she wasn't being earnest. When she was talking about something she really loved, she *glowed*.

'That all sounds fun.'

'We'll attract fans of Austen and the Regency,' she said. 'And that'll be the theme for the week. Craft workshops and decking the house out for Christmas, so visitors can feel part of the past.'

Feel part of the past. Now Sam understood her. This was clearly her favourite room in the house, and she must be devastated by the fact that this was the room with the problem. Now he could see why she'd blinked away tears.

'Forgive me for being dense, but I can't see any signs of mould,' he said. 'Isn't it usually black and on the ceiling?'

'This is white and it's behind the mirror that usually goes over the mantelpiece, but it's just come to the edge. You can see it under ultraviolet light.' She sighed. 'We'll have to take the hangings down to dry them out and then make sure we get all the spores.'

He walked over to the mantelpiece and put his fingers to the wall, and she winced visibly.

'Don't touch because of the mould?' he asked.

'Don't touch because of the oils on your fingertips, which will damage the silk,' she corrected.

'So this isn't wallpaper?'

'It's silk,' she said, 'though it's hung as wall-paper.'

'Pasted to the wall?'

'Hung on wooden battens,' she said. 'I'm guessing you haven't covered the care of textiles or paper on your course, then.'

He was going to have to come clean about this—at least partially. 'Now you've shown me round, why don't we talk about the job?' he asked.

'OK.' She led him through the house without commenting, but he could tell that she didn't take her surroundings for granted, she loved the place. It was her passion—just as he'd thought that fund management was his, but meeting Victoria had shown him that his feelings didn't even come close. Otherwise why would he feel perfectly fine about dropping everything to take over from his father?

Stockbroking wasn't his passion, either. He was doing this to make sure his father had a lot less stress in his life.

Did he even have a passion? he wondered. His best friend, Jude, lit up whenever Shakespeare was mentioned. Whereas Sam… He enjoyed the fast pace of his life, but there wasn't anything that really moved him or drove him. Since Olivia, he'd shut off from everything, lived just for the moment. He'd thought he was happy. But now he was starting to wonder. Was his father right and he was living in a useless bubble?

He shook himself and followed Victoria through a door in the panelling, and then down a narrow staircase.

'Shortcut—the former servants' corridors,' she said, and ushered him into a room that was clearly her office.

Everything was neat and tidy. Obviously she had a clear desk policy, because the only things on the gleaming wood were a laptop computer, a photograph, and a pot of pens. The walls were lined with shelves, and the box files on them were all neatly labelled.

'May I offer you some coffee?' she asked.

Right now he could kill for coffee. It might help him get his brain back into some semblance of order. 'Yes, please.'

'Are you a dog person or a cat person?' she asked.

That was a bit out of left field. Would it affect a potential job offer? 'I didn't grow up with either,' he said carefully, 'so I'd say I'm neutral. Though I'd certainly never hurt an animal.'

'OK. Wait here and I'll bring the coffee back. My dog's a bit over-friendly and he's wet—which is why he's in the kitchen,' she explained. 'How do you take your coffee?'

'Black, no sugar, thanks.'

'Two minutes,' she said. 'And perhaps you can email me your CV while I'm sorting coffee.' She took a business card from the top drawer of her desk and handed it to him. 'My email address is here.'

'Sure,' he said.

Samuel Weatherby was nothing like Victoria had been expecting. He was older, for a start—about her own age, rather than being an undergraduate or just applying for his second degree—and much more polished. Urbane. Although she wasn't one for fashion, she could tell that his suit and shoes were both expensively cut. Way outside the budget of the nerdy young student she'd thought he'd be.

So who exactly was Samuel Weatherby, and why had he come for this job?

She put the kettle on, shook grounds into the cafetière and made a fuss over Humphrey, who was still wet and muddy from the lake. While the coffee was brewing, she slipped her phone from the pocket of her jacket and checked her email. Samuel had sent over his CV—and it was nothing like what she'd expected. She was right in that he was her own age, but there was nothing even vaguely historical or PR-based on his CV. His degree was in economics and he worked as a hedge fund manager. Why would someone who worked in high finance, with a huge salary, want to take three months' work as an unpaid intern in a country house? It didn't make sense.

Frowning, she poured two mugs of coffee, added milk to her own mug, and was in the process of juggling them while trying to close the kitchen door when Humphrey burst past her.

'No, Humph—' she began, but she was much too late.

Judging by the 'oof' from her office, thirty kilograms of muddy Labrador had just landed on Samuel Weatherby's lap. Wincing, she hurried to the office and put the mugs on her desk. There were muddy paw prints all over Samuel's trousers and hair all over his jacket, and Humphrey was wagging his tail, completely unrepentant and pleased with himself for making a new friend.

'I'm so sorry,' she said. 'He's young—fifteen months—and his manners aren't quite there yet. He didn't mean any harm, and I'll pay your dry-cleaning bill.'

'It's fine.' Though Samuel made no move towards the dog. Definitely not a dog person, then, she thought. 'Thank you for the coffee.'

'Pleasure. I'm going to put this monster back in the kitchen.' She held Humphrey's collar firmly and took him back down the corridor to the kitchen. 'You are *so* bad,' she whispered. 'But you might have done me a favour—put him off working here, so I won't have to ask difficult questions.'

But, when she got back to her office, Samuel was the picture of equanimity. He wasn't on his feet, ready to make an excuse to leave; he looked perfectly comfortable in his chair.

She was going to have to ask the difficult questions, then.

'I read your CV while I made the coffee,' she said. 'And I'm confused. You're a hedge fund manager. A successful one, judging by your career history.' There had been a series of rapid promotions. 'Why on earth would you want to give up a career like that to do voluntary work?'

'A change of heart from a greedy banker?' he suggested.

Victoria wasn't quite sure whether he was teasing or telling the truth. Everyone always told her she was too serious, but she just wasn't any good at working out when people were teasing. Just as she'd proved hopeless at telling who really liked her for herself and who had their eyes on the money.

She played it safe and went for serious. 'You're not into historical stuff. You were surprised by some of the things I told you, which anyone who'd studied social history would've taken for granted; and I took you past artwork and furniture in the public rooms that would've made anyone who worked in the heritage sector quiver, stop me and ask more.'

Busted. Sam had just seen them as pretty pictures and nice furnishings.

Which meant he had nothing left to lose, because she obviously thought he wouldn't be right for the job. The truth it was. 'Do you want to know why I really want this job?' he asked.

She just looked at him, her dark eyes wary.

'OK. My dad really is your dad's stockbroker, and he talked to your dad to set up an interview for me.'

'But why? Is it some kind of weird bet among your hedge fund manager friends?'

That stung, but he knew she had a point. People in his world didn't exactly have great PR among the rest of the population, who thought they were all spoiled and overpaid and had a warped sense of humour. 'No. They're all going to think I'm insane, and so is my boss.' He sighed. 'This whole interview is confidential, yes?'

'Of course.'

'Good. Bottom line—and I need to ask you not to tell anyone this.' He paused. At her nod, he continued, 'My dad's not in the best of health right now. I offered to resign and take over the family business, so he can retire and relax a bit.'

'That's more logical than working here. Fund management and stockbroking have a lot in common.' Her eyes narrowed. 'Obviously he said no, or you wouldn't be here. Why do you want to be my intern?'

He might as well tell her the truth. 'Because Dad thinks I live in a bubble and doing this job for three months will prove to him that I can relate to ordinary people.'

'I'd say you're switching one bubble for another.' And, to her credit, her mouth was twitching slightly. So maybe she did have a sense of humour under all that earnestness and could also see the funny side of the situation. 'I've never met your dad, because my dad still handles the investment side of things here.' She looked straight at him. 'Does your dad think you can't take directions from a woman?'

'Possibly. To be fair, neither can he. I think he'll be driving my mum insane,' he said. 'Which is the other reason I want to come back to Cambridge. Dad has a low boredom threshold and I think she'll need help to get him to be sensible and follow the doctor's orders.'

'That,' she said, 'does you a lot of credit. But I'm not sure this is the right job for you, Samuel. You're way overqualified to be my intern, and frankly your salary is a lot more than mine. Even if you earn the average salary for your job—and from your CV I'm guessing you're at the higher end—your annual salary, pre-tax, would keep this house going for six months.'

It took him seconds to do the maths. It cost that much to run an estate? Staff, maintenance, insurance, taxes… Maybe he could help there and look at her budget, see if the income streams worked hard enough. 'Take my salary out of the equation. It's not relevant. What attributes do you need in your intern?'

'I want someone who can work on their own initiative but who's not too proud to ask questions.'

'I tick both boxes,' he said.

'Someone who understands figures, which obviously you do. Someone who's good with people.'

'I'm good with people,' he said. 'I have project management skills. I know how to work to a budget and a timeframe. I admit I know next to nothing about history or conservation, but I'm a fast learner.'

'I think,' she said, 'you'd be bored. You're used to living in the middle of London, with an insanely fast-paced job. Here, life's much slower.

If I gave you the job, you'd be unhappy—and that's not fair on you, or on the rest of my team.'

'If you don't give me the job, I'll be unhappy,' he countered. 'I want to be able to keep an eye on my dad. He's not going to retire until I prove myself to him. The longer it takes me to find a job where I can do that—even though, frankly, it's insulting—the longer he'll keep pushing himself too hard, and the more likely it is he'll have a full-blown stroke. This is about damage limitation. I have most of the skills you need and I can learn the rest. And I have contacts in London who can help with other things—publicity, website design, that sort of thing.'

She shook her head. 'I don't have the budget for provincial consultancy fees, let alone London ones.'

'You won't need it. I can call in favours,' he said. 'Give me the job, Ms Hamilton. Please.'

CHAPTER THREE

IN THE HALF-HOUR since they'd first met, Victoria had worked out that she and Samuel had next to nothing in common. He was all about figures and she was about words. He lived in the fast lane and she was more than happy to spend her life here in the country house where she'd grown up, curating the past.

But she needed help to raise funds, and he needed a job to make his father believe in him. As long as they could work together, giving him this job could solve a problem for both of them.

'Let's say a week's trial,' she said. 'See if we can work together.'

'Thank you,' he said.

'If you hate it here, that still gives me enough time to find another intern before things get really hectic.'

He inclined his head. 'And if you can't stand me, then you only have to put up with me for a week.'

'I wasn't going to be rude enough to say that.' But she'd thought it, and she could feel the guilty colour bursting into her cheeks.

'Lighten up. I was teasing, Vicky.'

'Victoria,' she corrected. Not that she'd offered to be on first name terms with him.

As if he'd read her mind, he asked, 'Do your staff normally call you Ms Hamilton?'

'No,' she admitted.

'But you prefer formality.'

'Nobody shortens my name. Why are you making it a problem?'

'I'm not.' He looked at her. 'I need to make friends with your dog and meet the rest of your team. At work tomorrow, would you prefer me to wear a suit or casual clothes?'

'The house is open for visitors tomorrow afternoon,' she said. 'But if you're meeting Humphrey...' She winced, seeing the mud smeared over his expensive suit.

'How about,' he said, 'I wear jeans in the morning so it doesn't matter if the dog covers me with mud, but I bring a suit for when the house is open? Or do your house stewards wear period costume?'

'You'll need training before you can be a steward. And we don't usually wear period dress. But I was thinking about it for the events on the Christmas week,' she added.

'Good idea,' he said. 'It would be an additional visitor attraction.'

She had a sudden vision of him in Regency dress and went hot all over. Samuel Wetherby could *definitely* be a visitor attraction. He looked good enough in modern dress; in Regency dress, he'd be stunning. She shook herself. 'Yes,' she said, striving to keep her voice cool and calm. 'OK. I'll see you tomorrow at nine. If you can give me your registration number, I'll make the sure the stewards know you're staff so they won't ask you to pay for parking.'

'Sure. Do you have paper and a pen?'

She took a notepad from her drawer and passed it to him. He scribbled the number down for her. 'Nine o'clock, then.'

'Nine o'clock—and welcome to the team.' She held out her hand to shake his, and when his skin touched hers it felt almost like an electric shock.

How ridiculous. She never reacted to anyone like this. And it was completely inappropriate to have the hots for her intern. Even if he was really easy on the eye—tall, with neatly cut dark hair, green eyes and a killer smile. To give herself a tiny bit of breathing space and remind herself that she was his boss for the next week, at the bare minimum, so she had to keep this professional, she took a copy of the house guide

book from the shelf behind her and handed it
to him.

'Bedtime reading?' he asked.

Bedtime. There was a hint of sultriness in his
tone. Was he doing this deliberately? A twinkle
in his eye made her think that he might be teasing her. And now she felt tongue-tied and stupid. 'I thought it might be useful background,'
she mumbled.

'It will be.' He smiled at her. 'Thank you for
giving me a chance.'

Honestly. He could have charmed his way
into any job, not just this one. Part of her wondered if it was some elaborate plot between her
parents and his to set them up together; but
of course not. A man as gorgeous as Samuel
Weatherby had probably been snapped up years
ago. Not that she was going to ask if accepting
this job would cause a problem with his partner.
She didn't want him to think she was fishing
for information. 'See you tomorrow,' she said,
hating that she didn't sound anywhere near as
businesslike as she should.

From hedge fund manager to intern. This next
bit of his life was going to be like the ancient
Chinese curse, Sam thought: *interesting.* He
sent a quick text to his mother to tell her he'd
got the job and was just nipping back to Lon-

don to sort out a few things but would be back later that evening. Then he hooked his phone up to the hands-free system in his car and headed back to London.

His first call was to his best friend.

'Bit early for you on a Sunday, isn't it, Sammy?' Jude asked.

'I'm in Cambridge, so I had an early Saturday night,' Sam explained.

'Is everything okay?'

'I'm not sure.' Sam filled him in on the situation.

'Oh, my God. I'm so sorry. How is your dad?'

'Grumpy. Worried sick and not admitting it. And I think Mum's patience with him is going to wear thin pretty quickly.' Sam paused. 'You'd do the same, wouldn't you?'

'Give up my career and move back home to keep an eye on my parents, you mean?' Jude asked.

'I was always going to come back to Cambridge and take over the firm from Dad,' Sam reminded him. 'It's just happening a bit sooner than I expected.'

'In your shoes, I'd do the same,' Jude said.

Which made Sam feel slightly better about his decision. 'I'm not putting the flat on the market until the spring, so I can rescue you from the dragon landladies and give you a key so you've got somewhere to stay for your West End run, if you like.'

'Are you sure?'

''Course I'm sure.'

'I can only afford to give you the going land-lady rent towards the mortgage,' Jude warned.

Sam knew that theatre actors didn't have the massive salary everyone thought they did. 'That's not necessary. I'll know the flat is being looked after rather than being left empty, and that's worth more than any rent. But I'm very happy for you to dedicate your first award win to me.'

Jude laughed. 'You could be waiting a while. Thanks. I accept. And you've more than earned that dedication.'

'I'm heading to London now, to pack. Come and pick up the keys at lunchtime.'

'Will do. And thanks again.' Jude paused. 'Have you told your boss?'

'Not yet. That's the next call.'

'Good luck with that.'

'It'll be fine,' Sam said, with a confidence he didn't quite feel.

'Are you *insane*?' was his boss's reaction when Sam told him he was resigning.

'No.'

'You were supposed to be visiting your par-ents for the weekend. And I know you haven't been headhunted, because that kind of news never stays secret for long. Why the hell are you resigning?'

'Confidentially, Nigel?' Sam asked. 'And I mean it. Not a word to anyone.'

Nigel sighed. 'All right. Tell me.'

'Dad was rushed into hospital this week. Mum didn't tell me until I got home. It was a mini-stroke and he seems OK now, but if he doesn't slow down he could have a full-blown stroke. I need to be here to keep an eye on them both.'

'Fine—then take a sabbatical until your father's well again.'

'I can't do that. It's permanent. I'm not coming back,' Sam said. 'If I'd been headhunted, I'd be on three months of garden leave with immediate effect, according to my contract.' Which gave him the three months in which he needed to convince his father that he wasn't reckless.

Then it hit him. Of course, his father would know about the clause giving three months' garden leave; that was obviously why Alan had specified three months working in an 'ordinary' job.

'You haven't been headhunted,' Nigel pointed out.

'But I'm going to take over the family business from Dad,' Sam said, 'so that counts as working in the same area and it's the same thing. I'm pretty sure HR will have me locked out of the computer system at work as soon as you tell them.'

'What do you want—a pay rise or more responsibility?' Nigel asked.

'Neither. This isn't a ruse to get more money or a promotion. I really do want to keep an eye on my parents.' The way both of them seemed to have aged twenty years overnight had shocked Sam. As their only child, he knew it was his responsibility to look after them—and, more than that, he *wanted* to take care of them. They'd always supported him. Now it was his turn to be supportive.

'You're serious, aren't you?' Nigel asked.

'Completely.' Sam knew that people in his world had a reputation for being shallow, but any decent person would do what he was doing. Wouldn't they?

Nigel coughed. 'Well, if things change, you'll always be welcomed back. And I hope everything goes all right with your dad.'

'Thanks. Do you need me to do any paperwork?'

'I'll sort it out with HR. Email me the address where you're staying so I can get the paper copies to you.'

'I will do. And thanks, Nigel. I know I'm dropping you in it and I appreciate it.'

'I guess at least you're not going to a competitor. And, as you said, you'd be on garden leave anyway.'

'If whoever takes over from me needs any advice or information, I'll be available,' Sam said.

'That's fair. All right. Well, good luck.'

'Thanks, Nigel.'

All bridges fully burned, Sam thought. He'd agreed a week's trial with Victoria; now he'd officially resigned, he needed to make sure the trial worked out so she let him stay on at Chiverton until his dad was ready for him to take over.

He stopped off at a supermarket to buy a box of nice biscuits and some fruit as a welcome for his new colleagues. Then he browsed in the pet section and bought a squeaky toy, tennis balls, and a bag of dog treats.

Back at his flat, he packed a suitcase and his laptop. The rest of the contents, once Jude had finished his West End run and was back in rep, could either go with the flat or to charity. Funny how little sentiment Sam had for his belongings. Then again, he really only used his flat as a place to sleep. He didn't have the same connection to the building that Victoria Hamilton had to Chiverton Hall.

When Jude arrived to collect the key, he insisted on taking Sam for lunch. And then Sam drove back to Cambridge. To his new life. And hopefully he could help keep his father in good health.

The next morning, at exactly five minutes to nine, the phone on Victoria's desk shrilled.

'Victoria Hamilton.'

'Samuel Weatherby, reporting for duty, ma'am.'

'I'll come and let you in,' she said. Humphrey trotted along beside her to the gate, his nose just ahead of her knee; she'd given up trying to make him walk to heel. 'I want you on your best behaviour,' she warned. 'If Samuel's a good intern, I want to keep him until after the ball.'

Humphrey gave her a look as if to say, 'And if he's not?'

'If he's not, you can run off with all his things and make him chase you right to the end of the park—and then do some judicious chewing,' Victoria said.

And oh, Samuel *would* have to look good in jeans. Faded jeans that fitted him perfectly, teamed with a mustard-coloured sweater she suspected might be cashmere and brown suede boots. His coat was expensively cut, and he was carrying a battered leather satchel and a carrier bag from a high-end supermarket.

'I left my suit and shoes in the car,' he said with a smile.

'I can sort out a locker for you, if you like,' she said.

'It's fine.' He eyed the Labrador. 'Right. First off, dog, you and I need to make friends.'

'His name is Humphrey,' she supplied.

'As in Bogart?'

She nodded. 'When he was a tiny pup, he looked like Bogart, all droopy jowls.'

'Humphrey, I come bearing gifts,' Samuel said. 'May I?' He produced a tennis ball from the carrier bag. 'Sit, and I'll throw it for you.'

'Better go further back in the grounds before you throw it for him,' Victoria said. 'The garden team has enough to do without Humphrey running across the flower beds and squishing the new plants.'

'Oh.' Samuel gave her a sheepish grin, and it made her tingle all over. 'I didn't think of that.' He glanced in the bag. 'What about a squeaky toy?'

She wrinkled her nose. 'That's really kind of you, but it'll take him less than three minutes to unpick all the stitching, unstuff it, and get the squeaker out. Then he'll shred what's left and spread it over three rooms.'

He grimaced. 'You can tell I know nothing about dogs. I bought him some treats as well, but I guess you'd better check they're suitable.

Though I did buy organic ones with no preservatives or gluten.'

He'd tried so hard. Victoria's heart melted. 'Thank you. I'm sure he'll love them.' She took pity on him. 'The way to make friends with him is to ignore him and let him come to you. No sudden movements, let him sniff you, and if he rolls over onto his back it means he likes you and he's expecting a tummy rub.'

Two minutes later, Humphrey was enjoying a thorough fuss. When Samuel stopped, Humphrey gave him an indignant look and waved his paw imperiously.

Sam grinned. 'You know what he's saying, don't you? "Play it again, Sam,"' he said in his best Bogart drawl.

Victoria didn't quite have the heart to correct him on the misquote. He was making such an effort. And his smile was so cute…

Not that she should be noticing how cute Samuel was. This was strictly business.

'OK. We've established you and Humphrey are going to get on.' Which was a big hurdle for her. If her dog didn't like her intern, it would make things really difficult. 'Just don't leave your lunchtime sandwich within his reach and unguarded, because Labradors are horribly greedy,' she warned. 'Coffee?'

'Yes, please. So what's the agenda for this morning?'

'I want to finalise what we're doing for Christmas week, then do a project plan for each event, costings and an overall critical path analysis.'

He looked at her as if she'd just grown two heads.

'What?' she asked.

'I wasn't expect—' He stopped himself.

'You weren't expecting me to be in the slightest bit businesslike?'

He winced. 'To be fair, when you showed me round yesterday it was clear how much you love this place. And in my experience that kind of feeling tends to blind people to financial practicalities.'

'Sadly, you can't run a house like this on love. You have to learn to juggle things—and you need to keep an eye on costs, without making the sort of false economies that'll cause you problems in the future.'

'Noted,' he said. 'So, your timeline. Do you already have a list of events?'

'Yes and no. I brainstormed a few things with my parents.'

'It might,' he said, 'be worth brainstorming with a complete outsider. Someone who doesn't know the limitations and might come up with something totally impractical that will spark off a more practical idea.'

'Is that your way of telling me you want to brainstorm with me?'

He smiled. 'Why don't I make the coffee? By the way, I brought a box of biscuits and some fruit to say hello to the rest of the team. And I picked up some biscotti this morning from the bakery round the corner from my parents, as it's my first day working here and I need to make a good impression on the boss.'

She wasn't sure whether he was teasing her or not. 'Thank you,' she said warily.

'It's an intern's duty to make coffee, so point me in the direction of the kitchen and I'll make it. Milk and sugar?'

'Just a splash of milk, please.' She showed him the kitchen and where everything was kept, then headed back to her office with Humphrey by her side.

Samuel came back with coffee and a plate of biscotti and retrieved the dog treats from his satchel. 'Are these OK?' he asked, handing her the packet.

'They're his favourites. He'll be your friend for life.' She looked at the dog, who was wagging his tail hopefully. 'Humphrey, sit.'

Humphrey sat.

'Paw,' she said.

Humphrey lifted one paw and gave Samuel a soulful look.

'Do I throw it to him?' Samuel asked.

'Yes, or you can leave it in your hand and he'll take it—though he might need reminding to be gentle.'

'I'm not scared of dogs. I know I sound stupid, asking, but none of my friends had dogs when I was growing up so I don't actually know how to act around them.'

The fact that he was admitting where he didn't have experience boded well for him working here and it reassured her. 'Would you say that to your dad?' she asked.

'If he asked me.'

She frowned. 'Then why does your dad think you're reckless?'

'Because my particular fund deals in high-risk investments.' He looked at her, his green eyes wide with sincerity. 'Which I wouldn't recommend to a client who wants a low-risk investment.' He shrugged. 'But I guess Dad's view of me might be a bit biased.'

'What did you do?' she asked, expecting him to say that he'd had a few speeding fines.

'I applied only to one university,' he said. 'Dad thought I was being stupid, not having a backup. But I didn't need a plan B because I knew I'd get my grades.'

She wasn't sure if she found his confidence more scary or sexy.

'And there's my car. Dad would prefer me to have a big four-by-four or a saloon car. Probably a grey one.'

'Don't tell me—yours is a red two-seater, low-slung and fast?'

'And convertible,' he said. 'And, yes, before you ask, I've had two speeding fines. But the last one was three years ago and it wasn't in this car. I've learned from my mistakes.'

Clever, capable, and charming. And the tiniest bit of a rogue, she thought. Women must fall for Samuel Weatherby in droves. She'd better make sure she wasn't one of them. Apart from the fact that her judgement in men was hopeless, she didn't have the time or the emotional space for it. She needed to concentrate on raising money for the ballroom restoration.

'Right. Brainstorm,' she said brusquely. 'We normally close the house to visitors from the middle of October through to February half-term, so we can clean properly and do any restoration work. But this year I want to open the house for the whole week before Christmas, maybe just the main rooms, and deck it out as it would've been in Regency times. I want to hold workshops for Christmas crafts, a dance class before the ball, and then a Regency costumed ball on the Saturday night with the kind of supper that would've been served during the Regency period.'

'Don't forget Santa for the little ones,' Samuel said.

She shook her head. 'If you mean Santa with his red suit and beard and ho-ho-ho, that's an American tradition and it didn't appear in England until the eighteen-fifties—which is way later than the Regency.'

'But if you're trying to attract family visitors, you know that the children will expect to see Santa,' he pointed out.

'This is a Regency Christmas,' she said, 'to go with the Regency ballroom.'

'So no Father Christmas.' He frowned. 'But you will at least have Christmas trees?'

She winced. 'In Regency times, Christmas trees were pretty much limited to the Royal family, after Queen Charlotte introduced her yew tree decked with almonds, raisins and candles in eighteen hundred. They didn't become popular among ordinary people until after a magazine drawing of Victoria and Albert's tree in 1848.'

'No Father Christmas and no Christmas trees. It doesn't sound like much fun. What did they actually do to decorate the house in Regency times, then?' he asked.

'Greenery and garlands.'

'Dull,' Samuel said. 'People will look at it and see what they're missing from today—proper Christmas trees and Santa.'

'Which are anachronistic,' she protested.

'Who cares?'

'I do, actually.' She frowned at him. 'Attention to detail is important.'

'OK, I get that you're a history fiend, but normal people don't really care if you're a few years out on a tradition,' he said. 'Isn't Christmas meant to be about fun?'

'Ye-es,' she said warily.

'Then ignore the fact that they're a few years out and use Santa and the Christmas trees,' he said. 'You already have things in the house that are modern—electric light and running water, for starters. You don't light the house with candles any more, do you?'

'Only because the insurance company would have a hissy fit.'

'Well, then. What's the problem with having modern Christmas traditions as well?'

Because then it wouldn't be a Regency Christmas.

Her dismay must have shown in her face, because he said, 'Lighten up a bit, Vicky.'

'My name is Victoria.'

He raised an eyebrow. '"Plain Victoria, and bonny Vic, and sometimes Tori the curst…"'

It was so out of left field that she wasn't sure she was hearing him correctly. Was he quoting Petruchio's speech at her, but substituting every variety of her own name instead of Kate?

He continued, '"Queen of Plum Hall, my super-dainty Vicky…"'

He *was*. Her eyes narrowed. 'Are you calling me a shrew?'

'Just trying a few different names,' he said, though his expression said that he knew perfectly well what he was doing.

'*Shrew* was one of my A-level texts. You didn't do English A level—' according to his CV, she remembered, he'd studied maths, further maths, economics and law '—but you're the same age as me. Did your girlfriend take English and make you test her on quotes or something?'

'No. I tested my best friend on his lines when he was at RADA.'

She ignored the fact that his best friend was an actor. So he *had* been calling her a shrew. 'I'm not difficult.' Though there were parallels between herself and Katherine: she was the elder daughter, and Lizzie had been so beautiful. And she was unmarriageable without the house as a dowry.

'You can call me a stool, if it makes you feel better.'

He clearly understood all the nuances of the phrase. 'It doesn't. I'm trying to take things seriously.'

'Maybe too seriously,' he said.

That stung, because she knew it was true. But why couldn't he understand how important this was to her? 'It's not a game. Do you have any idea how serious mould is in heritage settings? Fabric is incredibly vulnerable to damage.'

'And it's being fixed.'

'We're taking the wall hangings down this week to dry them.' She was dreading what else they might find.

'Can't you leave them where they are and just put more heating in the room to dry it out?'

'No. If you just add heat, the mould will grow like mad and feed off the fabric. It's humidity that we need to deal with,' she explained.

'OK. I promise to take this seriously,' he said. 'But I still think you need Santa and Christmas trees. They might be anachronistically wrong, but not to have them would be commercially wrong—and this is about raising money.' He paused. 'What else?'

'In Regency times they'd have a kissing ball.'

His eyes gleamed slightly. 'Ball as in dance?'

'Ball as in greenery,' she said. 'It's made from holly, ivy, rosemary and mistletoe.'

'Hence the kissing.' The gleam intensified, making her feel hot all over.

'Hence the kissing.' And how bad was it that she found herself wondering what it would be like to kiss Samuel Weatherby? To cover how flustered she felt, she buried herself back in historical detail. 'It'd be decorated with spices, apples, oranges, ribbons and candles.'

'Spices?'

'Cinnamon sticks, most likely,' she said. 'Maybe nutmeg. And they'd keep a Yule log burning—which we obviously can't do, for insurance reasons. And there would be sprigs of holly in every jug and spread across every windowsill.'

'No tinsel, then.'

'Absolutely no tinsel. And no Christmas cards—the first ones were Victorian, they weren't in colour and they didn't really become popular until the Penny Post was introduced.'

'Victorian.' He looked thoughtful. 'Why don't you make it a Victorian Christmas week, then? It'd be easier.'

'Because Regency costume is nicer than Victorian,' she said, 'and the ballroom furnishings are Regency.'

'And you're going to get everyone to dress up in Regency costume for the ball?'

She nodded. 'I need to think about whether to do the food as standing tables—a buffet, in modern terms—or seated tables in the dining room. I think tables would be nice, and we can have them set out in the Regency way—though I'm not going quite as far as the Prince of Wales and having a stream of fish swimming down the room.'

'Fish?' He sounded mystified.

'The Prince wanted to be known as the grandest host of all time. When he became Prince Regent, he held a ball for two thousand guests; there was a table in the middle of the room, two hundred feet long, with a stream, banks lined with flowers, and real fish swimming in it. There were sixty waiters—one of them in a full suit of armour—and the banquet went on until dawn.' She spread her hands. 'And two years later he had another ball where they served more than nine hundred different dishes.'

'That,' he said, 'is showing off and disgustingly extravagant.'

'Exactly. So mine's going to be more sensible. I'll still serve it *à la française*, so all the dishes will be laid out on the table and you tell the servers what you'd like. Soup and fish for the first course, meats and vegetables and custards and jellies for the second, and then the wafers and sponge biscuits with dessert wine, fresh fruit and sweetmeats. Actually, the Victoria Hamilton who lived here in the Regency era kept a very detailed diary, and I was planning on using things from her menus.'

The woman she was named after, perhaps? Sam looked at her. When she was talking about historic food like this, she *glowed*. This was clearly her passion. And it drew him.

'Is that what you would have done if you hadn't taken over from your dad?' he asked. 'Food history?'

'That or book conservation,' she said.

He could definitely see her among rare old books, all quiet and serious.

'What's so different about historical food?' he asked.

'The taste,' she said. 'As a student, I did a seminar in food in history, and our tutor did a workshop where we made Tudor sweetmeats. We made candied roses, marchpane and these Portuguese oranges—basically filled with a kind of marmalade—and the flavours were so intense.'

'Could you run a workshop like that, as part of Christmas events?' he asked.

'It's on my list of possibles. I thought people

might like to make Georgian stamped biscuits and sugar mice,' she said. 'And maybe violet and orange cachous.'

'Sounds good,' he said. 'What about outside? I know fairy lights aren't historical, but they'd mean you could open in the evenings, show people the garden as a kind of winter wonderland thing, and you could maybe have a kind of pop-up café offering mulled wine, hot chocolate, and hot snacks—say paninis and doughnuts. Oh, and definitely hot chestnuts as it's Christmas.'

'Cost it for me,' she said, 'and we'll discuss it.'

He blinked. 'Just like that?'

She shrugged. 'You're sensible. You know we're on a budget so it won't be all-singing, all-dancing and fireworks.'

'Fireworks?' He grinned. 'We *could*...'

'Cost it,' she said, rather than taking the bait and telling him they didn't have fireworks in Regency times. Or maybe they did. Not that he was going to ask her, right now.

She was clearly throwing him in at the deep end. That was fine by him. This was going to be a challenge—and he'd make sure it was also going to be fun. 'Do you have a list of approved suppliers, or can I just go wild?'

'I have a database,' she said. 'It's searchable

by name, location and goods or service. And I've included ones we won't ever use again, with a note as to why.'

'Did you design the database yourself?' he asked, suddenly curious.

'Yes.' She shrugged off the achievement. 'It was a bit quicker than our old index cards.'

A woman not to underestimate, then. 'OK. Do you want me to work in here with you?'

'If you don't mind sharing my desk,' she said.

Her desk was an ancient table, easily big enough for them to share. 'That's fine.'

'I'll just move some of my stuff, to give you some room,' she said.

Given that he'd noticed her clear desk policy yesterday, she hardly had to move a thing. But she did move a photograph of herself as a teenager, standing with another teen; it looked as if the picture had been taken in the grounds here.

'Who's this?' he asked, picking it up from the mantelpiece where she'd put it and looking more closely. 'Your best friend?'

'My little sister, Lizzie,' she said.

But there didn't seem to be a more recent photograph of them in the room. They didn't look much alike, either; Lizzie was several inches taller than Victoria, with a mop of blonde curls and blue eyes rather than dark hair and dark eyes like her sister's. Yet the way they were posing together, their arms wrapped around each other and clearly laughing, made it obvious that they were close.

'So Lizzie doesn't help to run the house or the garden?' he asked. 'Or is she still a student, off somewhere working on her PhD?'

Victoria sucked in a breath. 'No. She died six months after this picture was taken. Leukaemia.'

Sam flinched. He'd had no idea. Why hadn't his father warned him? 'I'm sorry. That must've been hard for you.'

'For all of us, especially Mum and Dad. But you were sort of right. Lizzie was my best friend as well as my sister.'

And now he had an inkling why she was so serious. Losing your younger sibling would be hard at any age, but especially so in your teens. 'How old were you?' he asked.

'I was fifteen and she was thirteen. Twelve years ago, now.' She looked straight at him. 'Lizzie loved Jane Austen and the Regency. The ballroom was her favourite room, too.'

So Victoria wasn't just saving the room for the house's sake: it was in memory of her beloved little sister.

No wonder she was so serious about it.

'The restoration—and the ball—will be a nice testimonial to her, then,' he said.

She nodded. 'And it's why I can't just be frivolous and fluffy about it. It needs to be *right*.'

'I get that, now,' he said. 'Though Lizzie doesn't look the type who'd want you to be all doom and gloom.'

'No. Lizzie was one of these really sunny people who always saw the sparkle. She'd love the idea of planning a Regency ball and a historical supper, based on the diary of the Victoria Hamilton who lived here in Regency times.'

'Life's short,' he said. 'You learned that with your sister. I'm learning that with my dad. And maybe we need to make the most of it and find the fun.'

'Gather ye rosebuds?' she asked dryly.

'Perhaps.' He looked at her. 'OK. I'll make a start on the costings for the trees and Santa, if you can log me into your database.'

'Thanks. Actually, I've already added you to the intranet. Your password's valid for this week.' She wrote it down for him. 'Let me know if you need any extra information.'

Even though he was busy making lists of what he needed and companies that could quote for the work, Sam found himself watching Victoria covertly. She absolutely wasn't his type. The women he dated were glamorous and high-maintenance, and they were all very clear that he was looking for fun and not to settle down.

Victoria was reserved and didn't seem in the slightest bit bothered that there was dog hair over her clothes, and she was definitely not the frivolous type. He had a feeling that it was a long, long time since Victoria Hamilton had had fun.

And there was definitely something about her. Something that drew him, that intrigued him and made him want to know more.

But he couldn't act on that attraction or on the urge to get to know her better and teach her to lighten up. This was only a temporary post and he was supposed to be her intern. He needed to concentrate on that and on proving himself to his father, he reminded himself sharply. OK, she wasn't like Olivia—but he still couldn't let himself get involved. For both their sakes.

CHAPTER FOUR

IT WAS WEIRD, sharing her office, Victoria
thought. She was quite used to people popping
in to see her or to make a fuss of Humphrey but
having someone in her space all the time that
morning felt odd.

She tried not to eavesdrop on Samuel's calls;
she didn't want him to think she was a micro-
manager, and besides they both knew that he
was way overqualified to be her intern. He'd
spent years working in finance, so getting
quotes and working out costings would be practically second nature to him. If he wanted her
input, he'd ask for it.

She'd sent a note round to her team to let them
know that Samuel was working with them for a
week, possibly longer, to help with the ballroom
fundraising. So of course everyone dropped in
to her office to meet him and say hello.

Samuel charmed every single one of them,
even the older and more guarded members of
the team. 'I brought biscuits and fruit as a way

of saying hello to everyone and I've put them
in the kitchen, so please help yourself,' he said.

Watching him with everyone, Victoria had to
admit that his people skills were excellent. He
listened: he paid attention and he made everyone feel important.

He charmed her parents, too, when they
dropped by to say hello. Though she noticed
that he didn't mention his father's health, so
clearly her own father wasn't aware of the situation with his stockbroker. Maybe Samuel was
worried that it would be bad for business if anyone knew about his father's mini-stroke, though
she rather thought that her father would be more
concerned about an old friend than panicking
about the safety of his investments.

By the end of the morning, she still hadn't
worked Samuel out. He was a mass of contra-
dictions. His father thought him reckless; yet he
was prepared to give up a high-profile job and a
massive salary so he could come home to keep
an eye on his parents. He was an only child, yet
he'd empathised with the loss of her sister. His
working life had been all about figures and pre-
dicting the future, yet he could quote obscure
bits of Shakespeare.

He still hadn't mentioned a partner, so was
he single? Was he a workaholic like herself, too
busy to bother with dating? But she couldn't

ask, because that would mean he could ask her personal questions, too—and she had a feeling that if she gave her stock answers he'd see right through them. She didn't want his pity. Didn't need it. She was quite happy with her life just the way it was.

All the same, she was glad when Nicola, the senior room manager in her team, offered to take him to work with the room stewards for the afternoon. Just so she could get her equilibrium back.

'See you tomorrow, boss,' Samuel said at the end of the day, after he'd helped the stewards to close up the house.

'Sure.' She smiled at him. 'Thanks for your help. And for the biscotti and Humphrey's treats.'

'Pleasure.' He raised an eyebrow. 'I'm beginning to get why this place is special.'

'Good.' If he fell in love with the house, then he'd go above and beyond to save the ballroom.

The tough day of the week was Tuesday: the day the hangings were coming down from the ballroom. Victoria was awake at stupid o'clock and walked through the ballroom, Humphrey at her side, before the sun rose. This was Lizzie's heritage, and she hadn't taken enough care of it. 'I'm sorry, Lizzie,' she whispered, feeling sick. 'I've let you down. And I've let Mum and Dad down.'

Humphrey whined and pushed his nose into her hand to comfort her.

'I'll fix it. Whatever it takes,' she said softly.

Felicity's team wore protective clothing and masks so they wouldn't breathe in the mould spores, and the ballroom was going to be out of bounds to everyone for a couple of days, to make sure there weren't mould spores in the air. On Friday morning, the room would get a thorough vacuuming—and she'd be the one to do it.

'You're going to need pictures of the hangings coming down for the website page,' Samuel said. 'Do you want me to take them for you?'

So she wouldn't have to face her favourite room being dismantled? 'Thank you,' she said, 'for being kind. But I need to face this. Humphrey, stay here, and don't chew anything,' she added to the dog.

'He'll be fine with me,' Samuel said.

The Labrador had taken a real shine to Samuel. Part of Victoria felt a bit miffed that her dog had seemed to switch his loyalties so fast; but then again it was good that Humphrey was behaving well and not chewing Samuel's laces or his car key.

'Thanks,' she said, and headed for the ballroom. Once in her protective clothing and mask, she went in to the ballroom.

Bereft of furniture, the carpet, the paintings and the mirrors, the room looked forlorn. And the bare wall over the mantelpiece where the first strip of silk was coming down made her feel sick. It felt as if part of her childhood had been stripped away with the hangings—the part she'd loved so much with her sister. Misery flooded through her.

'OK, sweetie?' Felicity asked, patting her arm.

'Yes.' It was a big fat lie, and they both knew it.

'The good news is that you don't have a problem with the wall, so you're not going to have to get a builder in.'

Building work in heritage properties was always super-slow and super-costly, because there were so many regulations. She was glad that was one burden she didn't have to face.

'If we can't repair it well enough once it's properly dry and we've got rid of the mould, we've got the specialist weaving company on standby,' Felicity said. 'It's going to be fine.'

'Of course.' Victoria did her best to look and sound professional. And she took photographs of the wall as each strip came down, as well as photographing the silk itself, until the whole wall was bare.

When she got back down to her office, intending to make a start on the restoration project page for the website, Samuel stood up.

'You wanted an intern who uses his initiative, you said.'

She frowned. 'Yes.'

'Good. I'm taking you out to lunch,' he said.

She shook her head. 'That's kind, but I have a lot to do.' And burying herself in work had always helped in the past, when she was miserable.

'Delegate some of it to me,' he said, 'and let's get out of here. Just for an hour or so. Felicity's team has everything under control upstairs; the house isn't open this afternoon, so you can justify a lunch break.'

'I—'

'No arguments,' he said, not letting her even get the beginnings of an excuse out.

The fight went out of her. He was right. At this point, she could do with being away from here so she could get herself back under control.

'I'm driving,' he added. 'Get whatever you need. We're going out.'

There was no bossiness in his tone, just decisiveness. And a hint of sympathy. She picked up her handbag, put her phone in it, and grabbed her jacket. 'I'm guessing you're not planning on going somewhere dog-friendly?'

'No, but I'll scrounge some leftovers for Humphrey.'

'I'll go and leave him in my flat, then. Back in a tick.'

She settled the dog in his bed, then went back to the office and followed Samuel out to his car.

'Keep your coat on. It's cold, but the sun's shining. Roof down,' Samuel said.

Showing off?

But she had to admit that it was fun, driving with the cold air on her face while her feet were still warm. And he was a much more sensible driver than she'd expected.

'Lunch,' he said, parking at a country pub. 'I'm buying. No arguments.' He shepherded her inside, completely oblivious to the way every female head swivelled in his direction and then gave her a surprised look, as if wondering what someone as gorgeous as him was doing with someone as plain and ordinary as her.

Then he charmed the waitress into giving them a table near the open fire and perused the menu. 'Comfort food. Chicken Dijon with mashed potatoes and buttered kale sounds good to me. And don't tell me you don't feel like eating. Of course you don't. But this will help. Promise.'

She ordered the same as him. He didn't push

her to talk, but the food was fabulous and he was right about lunch making her feel better.

'Thank you,' she said.

He tipped his head slightly to one side. 'My pleasure. I know this ballroom thing's hard for you, but the silk's being looked after and today's going to be the worst day.'

'Unless I fail to get anything at all from the heritage fund,' she said, 'and the damage is worse than Felicity thinks it is, in which case we'll have to sell artwork. Which will break Dad's heart, because he loves every single painting in the house.'

'You've got costings for the worst-case scenario. And you're not the sort to give up. You're not going to have to sell any artwork. You'll get funding—plus there's the fundraising stuff we're working on.'

Strange how much it warmed her when he said 'we're'.

'I guess,' she said. 'I have a lot of memories of Lizzie in that room. We both loved it.'

'The memories will always be there,' he reminded her. 'And, OK, the room's going to look weird for a while, but in three months' time this will all be over and it'll look just as it always did. Plus you get to hold your costumed ball in there, just in time for Christmas.'

Without Lizzie. Every so often, something

came out of left field to make Victoria miss her little sister dreadfully. This was just one of those moments. Lizzie would've loved all the dressing up and the music and the dancing. She would've enjoyed helping to choose the food, too. And Victoria would've enjoyed sharing it with her sister.

Her thoughts were clearly written over her face, because he said softly, 'Your sister will be there in spirit.'

'Yes. She will.'

Samuel made her eat pudding, too. Treacle sponge with custard. She was going to have to take Humphrey for a longer run than usual every day for the next week, to burn off all the extra calories—but Samuel was right. This helped.

'Better?' he asked when she'd finished her coffee.

She nodded. 'Thank you. Much. But I should pay for lunch. I mean, you're my intern.'

'Doesn't matter. My old salary—which I'm still being paid, by the way, as I'm officially on garden leave—is a lot more than yours. Plus this was my idea, so it's my bill.' His gaze met hers, and suddenly there was an odd feeling in the pit of her stomach.

'Tell you what—you can buy me lunch later in the week, if it makes you feel better.'

Which felt like planning a date, and it sent her into a spin. 'Won't your partner mind?' The words were out before she could stop them. How horrific. Now he'd think she was fishing—either for information about his private life, or for confirmation that this was an actual date, and she wasn't sure which one was the most embarrassing.

'No partner,' he said easily. 'And if yours minds, tell him it's a business lunch.'

Not a date.

Not that a man as stunningly beautiful as Samuel Weatherby would want to date her. He must have women falling at his feet every single day. A plain, over-serious woman like her—well, Paul had made it clear that the only reason a man would be attracted to her was Chiverton Hall.

Her tongue felt as if it was glued to the roof of her mouth. 'Uh-huh,' was about all she could manage to say.

Great. Now he'd think she had the hots for him.

Maybe she should invent a partner.

But then he might mention her 'boyfriend' to her parents, and things would get way too complicated. Better to keep it simple. 'No partner, and this is a business lunch.'

'Indeed,' he said.

And how bad was it that his smile made her knees go weak?

To her relief, he didn't push her to talk while he drove her back to Chiverton. Humphrey was thrilled to see them, and Felicity's team had left; but Felicity had left a note on Victoria's desk, together with a box file.

Found these behind the hangings. Thought you might enjoy them.

She opened the box file, glanced through the contents and exclaimed in delight. 'Look at this! We already know when the room was turned into a ballroom, because we have Victoria Hamilton's diary. But here's a dance card, and some sheet music. I wonder how they got behind the hangings?'

'No idea,' he said. 'But I'd say it's worth photographing for your restoration page.'

She nodded. 'And maybe a display case, later on.'

'What's a dance card?' he asked.

'A booklet, really, where ladies could record who they were dancing with for each dance. Before Regency times, dancing was super-formal and one couple had to go all the way down the set and back again, so it could take half an hour for just one dance. And there was a really strict hierarchy as well—but things became a bit more fluid in Regency times and the dances were shorter. People brought dance cards back from Vienna and they became really fashionable,' she explained. 'Some of them were really pretty—they looked like fans, and there might be a ribbon to attach it to your wrist.' She examined the sheet music again. 'This is in three-four time. Waltz.' She grinned. 'So our Victoria was a little bit fast, then.'

He blinked. 'Fast?'

'Not quite Lady Emma Hamilton,' she said. 'No relation, either. But the waltz was considered a bit indecorous. Even Byron wrote a poem against waltzing.' She shrugged. 'But it was super-fashionable.'

Victoria was glowing again and she'd lost that hunted look she'd had earlier, Sam thought.

He'd suggested getting away while the silk was being taken out of the house because he could see how much she hated the situation. He'd intended to be kind; but it had turned into something more than that. He'd been so aware of her—how her dark eyes had golden highlights in them when she was interested about something, and how her mouth had a perfect Cupid's bow.

Which was ridiculous.

Victoria Hamilton wasn't his type. She was way too earnest and serious. She was the sort of woman who'd expect for ever, not just for fun.

Yet she'd asked him about his partner.

Their relationship was strictly business, so if he *had* been dating someone he couldn't see how having lunch with Victoria would be a problem. And she'd looked surprised when she'd asked him. Had her question been inadvertent, then? And did that mean she was interested in him?

Though she'd neatly sidestepped his own question at first. It made him wonder why; but if he asked her then it might become an issue.

Instead, he made a fuss of the dog. 'Well, that all sounds good. Something to put in a press release, anyway.' He smiled at her. 'I'm going to talk to the garden team.' He wanted to find out their views about lighting up the grounds, what was practical and how he could organise the power supply. And also it would put enough distance between himself and Victoria so he could remind himself that she was absolutely out of bounds.

On Friday, Samuel presented Victoria with a folder. 'Costings and project outlines,' he said.

'OK. Talk me through them.'

'Christmas trees,' he said. 'We want a huge

one in the courtyard and several in the house.
I've got a deal with a local supplier. He gives
us a very nice discount, and we allow him to
mention that he's our official supplier this year
in his promotional material.'

'Uh-huh.'

'Obviously we need lights, and I'm assuming you can't do traditional candles because of
the fire risk. I did start researching Christmas
decorations, but I thought that's more your thing
so I haven't included costings or suggestions.'

'OK,' she said.

'Give me a list of what you want, and I'll sort
out the sources and costings,' he said.

'I'll do that for this afternoon,' she said.

'Good. Next, staff,' he said. 'Obviously you
have the house stewards, the ones with all the
knowledge. But, if you want to make this real
for people, you need staff in Regency dress.
Tableaux. I was thinking six footmen and six
maids should be enough, and they'll also be able
to act as waiting staff at the ball.'

'It sounds wonderful,' she said, 'but I don't
have the budget to hire actors. Even if we can
talk volunteers into it, we'd still need costumes.'

'No budget needed,' he said. 'I'm calling in
favours, remember? They'll all bring their own
costumes; in return, the people who make the
costumes get photographs on their website and

yours, with credit, and the actors can include this on their CVs and use photographs on their own social media.'

'You've talked actors into doing this for nothing?'

He nodded. 'They're all willing to learn any lines you might want, or to improvise.'

'How did you manage this?' she asked, astonished.

'It's a quid pro quo,' he said. 'They get experience of working in Regency costume, which they can use if they're auditioning for costume dramas or films. They're all people who trained with my best friend.'

She remembered him talking about his best friend learning lines from Shakespeare. 'So is your best friend well-known?'

'In theatrical circles, yes. He's going to be huge. Jude Lindsey.'

It wasn't a name she recognised, but she didn't get to the theatre in London very often nowadays. Though she was impressed by Samuel's clear loyalty towards his friend. 'OK.'

'Outside lights, I've talked to the garden team, and we've come up with a lighting plan. I can walk you through it outside, if you like. I've sourced lights we can hire at a very cheap rate for up to a fortnight, and it's the same deal as the Christmas trees—they get to mention that they're our official sponsors, and we name-check them on our website and on all publicity material.'

He had far more chutzpah than she did; it was hardly surprising that he'd done so well. She would've struggled. 'That's all great. Thank you.' She paused. 'Did you go for fireworks in the end?'

'Sadly, they're out of budget,' he said. 'But maybe you could hold a concert in the grounds in the summer, with fireworks at the end—they'd look great reflected in the lake. And you could have pop-up food stalls.'

'It's a good thought,' she said. 'That's all really useful. And I owe you lunch and a quick chat.'

'An appraisal?' he asked.

'Something like that. Though it goes both ways. Do you like Italian food?'

'Yes.'

'Good. And I'm driving. Give me twenty minutes to assimilate this.'

'OK. I'll go and annoy the garden team,' he said. 'I'm scrounging cuttings and advice for my mum. I hope that's OK?'

'Of course,' she said with a smile.

His paperwork was impeccable. She didn't need him to walk her through the outdoor lighting scheme, because he'd mocked up photographs and marked up a copy of the visitor map. No wonder he'd been promoted so quickly as a hedge fund manager. He thought on his feet.

Once they were settled at their table in the Italian restaurant in the next village and they'd ordered lunch, she looked at him. 'First of all, your ideas are excellent. I have no idea how you sweet-talked everyone into offering you such amazing deals, but I'm very grateful. From my point of view, you've been a brilliant intern and frankly I think you're more than capable of doing *my* job, let alone the intern's.'

He inclined his head. 'Thank you.'

'I can't afford you as a consultant and I feel horrible about asking you to stay on until after the ball, without paying you anything.'

'So does that mean I don't get the job?'

'No. It means I feel guilty.'

He spread his hands. 'I knew the score when I accepted the week's trial.'

'So,' she said. 'The appraisal goes both ways. Your turn.'

'From my point of view, running events in a country house is nothing like what I do. It's like stepping into a different world. There are restrictions—which obviously there are in finance as well, but I'm surprised everything is so hidebound.'

Including the person who managed the house,

who wanted everything to be as historically accurate as possible—except he was too polite to say so, she thought.

'But I'm enjoying it,' he said. 'We're talking until Christmas, right?'

'Three months' voluntary work,' she confirmed.

'I'm on three months' garden leave,' he said. 'Which means I can't take a job in any kind of financial services, including my dad's company. And I'm still being paid. So it's not as if I'm a starving student who has to rely on his parents' support. Working for you means I have a valid excuse for living with my parents and keeping an eye on them—but it also means I'm not with them twenty-four-seven, which I think would end up with all of us wanting to murder each other. And it also means I'm proving myself to my dad.'

'Carry on like this, and your reference will be glowing so much they'll see it from the space station,' she said.

'Thank you.' He smiled at her.

She had a feeling there was something more. 'But?'

'Can I be honest?'

He was going to turn her down. She ignored the sinking feeling of disappointment. 'Of course.'

'You need to lighten up,' he said. 'Worry less.'

She'd heard that before. 'It's who I am,' she said.

'Here's the deal. I work with you on the Christmas week events, and you let me teach you how to have fun.'

'That,' she said, 'sounds just a bit worrying. Especially when you told me that your own father thinks you're reckless.'

'Was I reckless when I drove you or when I put together the garden plan?'

'No.'

'Well, then. Those are my terms.'

'So that makes me your pet project?'

He shrugged. 'Take it or leave it.'

Even though she thought he was being a tiny bit patronising, she needed his help with the restoration funding. Without him on board, she might not get the deals he'd negotiated. She certainly wouldn't get the servants in Regency livery. She didn't really have a choice. And she wasn't going to admit to herself that she was rather enjoying having him around.

'I'll take it,' she said. 'Welcome to the team.'

'Thank you.' He raised his glass of water. 'So here's to having fun.'

'Here's to restoring the ballroom,' she said.

'And having fun.'

He'd left her no way out. 'And having fun.'

CHAPTER FIVE

'Fun,' Victoria said on Monday morning. 'That's what this week will be about.'

Samuel gave her a suspicious look. 'Define fun.'

'Christmas decorations,' she said.

'You've already told me about those,' he said with a sigh. 'They're not fun in the slightest. Greenery, holly and a mistletoe ball. No sparkle, no ho-ho-ho, no nothing.'

'As we're having semi-anachronistic Christmas trees,' she said, 'we need decorations for them.'

'Tinsel!'

She narrowed her eyes at him. 'You know perfectly well tinsel's ana—'

'—chronistic,' he finished with a grin.

She ignored him. 'I think they need to match the decor of the room they're in. So we'll have red baubles and taffeta ribbons in the dining room. The one by the staircase needs to be all gold—we can gather pine cones from the estate and dried allium heads, which we can spray-paint gold.'

'Because of course spray paint was available in Regency times,' he said dryly.

'You're the one who's all about anachronism,' she reminded him. 'Dried alliums and peacock feathers will make stunning centrepieces for the mantels or the table.'

'Aren't peacock feathers supposed to be unlucky?'

She shrugged. 'We have a late Victorian bedroom here with original wallpaper—the famous Liberty peacock one,' she said.

'Famous?'

'Sometimes I feel as if I'm fifty years older than you.' She sighed. 'Come with me and I'll show you. Humphrey, stay, because I don't want muddy paw prints on the counterpane. It's an original, which is way too fragile to go in the washing machine.' She showed Samuel up to the small bedroom with its glorious turquoise, gold and navy wallpaper. The same print was on the counterpane on the wrought iron bed, the drapes were plain blue to match the background of the wallpaper, and the wooden shutters were painted the same turquoise as the wallpaper.

'Wow,' he said. 'I wasn't expecting this. It looks almost modern.'

'Timeless elegance,' she said. The wrought

iron bedframe had been painted ivory and gold, the lamps on the chests of drawers next to the bed had cream silk shades, and next to the fireplace was a wooden trolley containing a cream washstand set. The fireplace was black leaded and had a set of fire irons beside it.

'You can really imagine a guest at a house party staying here,' he said.

She nodded. 'It's my favourite room in the main house, after the ballroom and the library. I love the peacock feathers.'

'And that's why you're having them in the centrepieces.' He frowned. 'How do you even get peacock feathers? I haven't seen any peacocks in the ground.'

'Florist suppliers,' she said. 'The feathers are steam-cleaned. We have a rota of volunteers who do the floral arrangements in the house—in exchange, they get flowers from our garden to use at home. One of them's bound to know who to contact, and I'm hoping I can talk them into running a couple of workshops on Christmas wreaths and arrangements.'

'Sounds good,' he said. 'What other workshops are you planning?'

'There's a local artist who sells her stained glass in our shop,' she said. 'I'm hoping she'll run a couple of workshops on making a stained-glass tree ornament. Plus the Regency Christmas sweetmeats—the local sweet maker who supplies our shop will hopefully agree to do that. Then there's the Regency dance class and the ball.'

'If you're recreating the ball from Victoria's diary, maybe you should publish a transcription of the diary,' he said thoughtfully.

'I'd love to do an edition,' she admitted. 'But I don't have the time right now.'

'Delegate more to me to give you some time,' he suggested.

She smiled. 'That's nice of you to offer, but I think Victoria's diary could be my research rabbit hole. Once I start, you might not see me again for months.'

What did it feel like to be so passionate about something? Sam wondered. Part of him envied her. Keeping everything light meant he never really connected with anything.

'OK. So this week we're planning Christmas decorations,' he said.

'And a couple of trial runs, so we can see how long it takes to make them. We need to dry orange slices and either source or make snow-flakes, plus dry the alliums and spray-paint them and the pine cones.' She gave him a wry look. 'You're the one who was on about fun. Don't back out on me now.'

'I'm not backing out. Though I probably haven't done anything artistic since infant school,' he warned.

'That's OK. And it might impress your dad.'

Sam wasn't convinced. 'Uh-huh. What else?'

'The ball. We need to book someone to run a Regency dance class—the steps aren't the same as modern ballroom dancing—and call the dances in the evening,' she said. 'Plus a string quartet. As you have contacts in the acting world, do you have musician friends as well?'

He shook his head. 'The dance teacher will probably know someone. Or it might be worth talking to the university.'

She looked thoughtful. 'That's a good idea. My old college had a really strong music department. I could call them.'

'You were at Cambridge?' Though he didn't know why he was so surprised. He already knew she was bright. 'What made you choose Cambridge over Oxford?'

She shrugged. 'It meant I could live here and keep an eye on Mum and Dad.'

So she hadn't had the full student experience, the way he had, living away from home and having the space to find out who you were. He didn't have to ask why she'd felt she needed to look after her parents; it had been only a few years after her sister's death. Now he knew why she'd been so understanding about why he wanted to keep an eye on his own parents. She'd already been there. 'Call them,' he said. 'What else?'

'Food. I've been working on the menu, based on Victoria's diary. My best friend, Jaz, is a food historian, so I'm hoping to get her students involved.'

'You could get a lot of interest from magazines if you wrote an article about a Regency Christmas dinner. They'll be planning the Christmas issue about now,' he said.

'Planned them already and putting them to bed, more like,' she said. 'Anyway, it's not a Christmas dinner. It's a ball supper.'

'Even so. You'll need to do a trial run on the food, so you could set up a table here. If we're careful with the angle, it won't matter if there isn't a Christmas tree in shot.'

'Do you have any magazine contacts?' she asked.

'No.' He shrugged. 'OK. So that's decorations, workshops, food and the ball itself. What about costume? Do you have a Regency dress?'

'I do, but it's a day dress rather than a ball gown. Meaning it's lawn rather than silk,' she explained.

He grinned. 'I would say, Cinderella, that you shall go to the ball—except obviously you're organising it so of course you'll be there, plus you're the daughter of the house rather than the one who'd been forced to be a skivvy.'

'Watch who you're calling an ugly sister,' she said. Her tone was light, but Sam had noticed her flinch.

'What did I say?' he asked.

'Nothing.'

'Victoria.' He took her hand. 'I was teasing. In my ham-fisted way, I was trying to say I thought it might be nice to sort out our costumes together. If you don't mind me going to the ball with you, and obviously I'll buy a ticket.'

'Uh-huh.'

He sighed. 'Tell me. Please. So I don't put my foot in it again.'

The thing that gnawed away at her, the thing that pushed her to try harder and harder.

'Tell me,' he said softly.

He was still holding her hand.

Her voice felt cracked as she whispered, 'I kind of am Cinderella. I'm adopted.'

He looked at her. 'You're still the daughter of the house. From what I can see, you parents adore you. Your dad spent ages in the garden with me last week, singing your praises.'

'It's not…' She dragged in a breath. 'Mum and Dad didn't think they could have children.

They tried IVF, but it didn't work out. So they adopted me—and then Mum fell pregnant with Lizzie. They've never, ever made me feel less than theirs or less important than Lizzie; but I've always thought that if they had to lose a daughter, it should've been me, not her, because she was their real daughter.'

'That's survivor guilt talking,' he said. 'And you're not being fair to yourself.'

'I promised Lizzie when she was dying that I'd look after them. Look after the house. Be the Hamilton daughter.' She swallowed hard. 'The house would've gone to Lizzie, because she was Mum and Dad's biological daughter, and I was fine with that. But then…' She closed her eyes for a moment and looked away, unable to bear the pity in his face. 'Lizzie died. Which left us all in limbo. Dad unpicked all the legal stuff so the house would go to me rather than to the nearest male relative, but it's not really mine. I'm the custodian.'

'Listen to me.' His voice was very soft. 'You are most definitely the heir to the house and it definitely belongs to you. You're the heart of this place. It doesn't matter about biology. You love this place and this family, and that's what's important.'

'Uh-huh.' She blew out a breath. 'But that's why…'

'Why you're so serious and earnest all the time, because you feel you owe your parents a debt and you have to work three times as hard as anyone else, to prove you're worthy of the Hamilton name.'

She stared at him, shocked that he'd understood without her having to explain. 'Yes.'

'Newsflash,' he said. 'You *are* worthy. And if your little sister loved you even ten per cent as much as you clearly loved her, she would've hated to see you beating yourself up like this.'

Humphrey chose that moment to bark.

'Even your dog agrees with me,' he said. 'You're more than good enough to do this.'

And he was still holding her hand.

This time, she met his gaze head-on. His green eyes were filled with sincerity—and something else she couldn't quite put her finger on. Shockingly, she found herself leaning towards him and her lips parting slightly. He was leaning towards her, too. For a second, she thought he was actually going to kiss her. And oh, how much she wanted this.

But then Humphrey barked. Samuel dropped her hand as if he'd just been scalded and took a backward step.

Two seconds later, there was a rap on her open door. 'Victoria?'

She forced a smile. She liked the senior room

manager very much, but right now she felt as if she'd just made a fool of herself. And she was grateful that Nicola hadn't witnessed it. 'Hi, Nicola. What can I do for you?' she asked rather more brightly than she felt.

'Just checking that you're happy with the steward rota for this week.' Nicola smiled at her.

She hadn't had time to look at it. But Nicola knew what she was doing. 'It's fine.'

'Good. Sam, are you joining us at all this week? I haven't put you in the rota, but I can fit you in anywhere you like.'

Samuel gave her his most charming smile. 'Although I'd love to, I think the boss has plans for me, this week—something to do with alliums, pine cones and spray paint.'

'Shame. You had all the ladies eating out of your hand—he hand-sold a dozen cream teas the other day, you know,' Nicola added to Victoria.

'Good for the café, then,' Victoria said, making an effort to recover her equilibrium.

'One thing, though. I didn't like to correct you in front of visitors, Sam, but I'm not sure our scone recipe really is originally from Chiverton,' Nicola confided.

'Maybe,' Victoria said, 'I should take a look at Victoria's diary and see if there's anything there. I was planning on using some of her rec-ipes for the ball, anyway.'

'On behalf of the stewards,' Nicola said, 'we'd be very happy to be guinea pigs for anything you want to try making beforehand.'

'Sounds like fun,' Samuel said. 'We could have a Georgian lunch party, maybe. Or an early dinner after the garden closes, so the garden team can be part of it, too.'

'What a good idea,' Nicola said.

The idea was gathering momentum; although Victoria could say no, she didn't want to sour the atmosphere. 'Thursday next week, then,' she said. 'Though I need a sous-chef.' She gave Samuel a pointed look.

'My cooking skills aren't advanced enough.' He held up both hands in a gesture of surren-der. 'When I hold dinner parties, it's either out at a restaurant or I get caterers in.'

'Time you broadened your skill set, then, young man,' Nicola said with a grin. 'Anything we need to know about, Victoria?'

'The information boards for the ballroom should be arriving at some point today. And I've checked the mould levels in the room—it's all fine.'

'Grand. I'll see you later,' Nicola said with a smile, and disappeared.

'I really don't cook,' Samuel said. 'Unless you count shoving something into the microwave.'

'You're the one who suggested holding a trial run of the supper,' she reminded him. 'And didn't you tell me to delegate stuff to you?'

'Not cooking. Unless you want to go down with food-poisoning,' he retorted.

'Microwave meals,' she said, rolling her eyes.

'There's nothing wrong with them. Anyway, you still live with your parents. Does your mum cook for you?'

'Sometimes; and sometimes I cook for my parents. Technically, right now you're living with yours,' she pointed out, 'so you're not in a position to criticise.'

'I'm not criticising.' He looked at her. 'Really. I don't cook.'

'We'll do it Regency style,' she said. 'Though I'll use a modern oven, the rest of it will be by hand.'

His eyes glittered. 'You said this week's going to be about fun.'

'It is.'

'Hmm. I bet Mr Darcy never had to cook anything.'

'You,' she said, 'are not Mr Darcy.' Though she had a feeling that he'd look absolutely stunning in Regency costume. To get her wayward thoughts under control, she resorted to briskness. 'Right. Jaz gave me the name of a woman who makes period costumes—Mrs Prinks—and the costumes on her website look really good, so I'd like to make an appointment with her to organise a dress.'

'Does she do men's costumes as well?'

'Yes.'

'Then we should go together,' he suggested. 'Is Mrs Prinks her real name?'

'I'd guess it was her business name,' Victoria said. 'If you can organise an appointment with her, I'll contact the man who teaches Regency dance in Cambridge and see if Jaz can fit us in this week. And, after we've organised all that, we're going to make Georgian biscuits.'

'Right.' His eyes narrowed. 'And I get decent coffee for being a kitchen serf?'

'Decent coffee,' she promised. 'And you also get to charm the stewards this afternoon by offering them something to have with their cup of tea that you made with your own fair hands.'

It didn't take long to sort out all the meetings. 'It's a pity that we couldn't have done both London trips on the same day,' she said.

'We could stay in London on the night between,' he said. 'At my flat.'

'Your flat.' She thought of that almost-kiss and went hot all over.

'I have a spare bedroom,' he said, 'so that wasn't a proposition.'

And how embarrassing that she'd thought that—albeit only for a nanosecond. 'It's a sensible suggestion. Thank you. I accept,' she said briskly. 'Right. I'll divert the office phone to my mobile. My kitchen awaits.'

'How do you know you've got the ingredients?' he asked.

'Shortbread biscuits and the like have been around for more than a thousand years,' she said. 'The recipes haven't changed that much over the years.'

'Are you telling me you've got a recipe for biscuits made a thousand years ago?'

'Not exactly, but I can make you fourteenth-century gingerbread from *The Forme of Cury*.'

'Curry?' He looked mystified.

'*Cury*. From the French *cuire*, to cook,' she said. 'Though it's not quite like the cakey gingerbread you get today.' She was glad of the safety of historical research. Where she wouldn't have to think about Samuel Weatherby and what it would be like if he kissed her. 'Think yourself lucky I'm not suggesting you make Roman honey cakes with a hand whisk. Jaz and I did that as undergraduates and you wouldn't believe how long it took to get the honey and eggs to the right texture.'

* * *

Sam was intrigued. What would Victoria's flat be like? He was guessing it would be as neat and tidy as she kept the office, but would it be as impersonal? Or would it give him more of a clue to the woman who'd surprised him earlier by her lack of confidence?

She led him through one of the servants' corridors—clearly this was a shortcut she'd been using for a long time—and then into her flat. Like the rest of the house, the rooms had high ceilings and large sash windows. The living room was almost entirely given over to books, though there was a comfortable-looking sofa and a small television in the corner. 'My room,' she said, indicating a closed door. 'Bathroom, if you need it. And the kitchen.'

The layout was incredibly old-fashioned—a butler's sink, which overlooked the lake, open shelving full of Kilner jars, a dresser with what he guessed were antique china plates, a scrubbed pine table with four chairs—but with a very modern oven. He blinked at it. 'Shouldn't you have an Aga or something?'

'Nope. Mum doesn't, either. I like the open, old-fashioned kitchen layout, like the nineteenth-century one we have on show downstairs, but I also love my modern oven.' She opened a drawer, took out an apron and handed it to him.

'You seriously expect me to wear a floral pinny?'

'If you're as much of a novice in the kitchen as you claim to be, you'll end up covered in flour without it.'

'As long as you don't take photographs and stick them on your website,' he grumbled.

She looked thoughtful. 'Experiments in Georgian cooking... Actually, you're pretty enough to get us a lot of hits.'

'*Pretty?*' This was outrageous.

And then he realised that the most earnest and serious woman he'd ever met was teasing him. And that he was more than tempted to extract a forfeit in the form of a kiss.

Which wasn't a good idea.

He needed to focus.

'Right.' He put the apron on.

'If you dressed as Mr Darcy, we could pose this in the kitchen downstairs,' she said. 'And then it could go on the website. Floral pinny being optional.'

'No,' he said.

'Fine.' She took some old-fashioned scales from the dresser, a large earthenware bowl from the cupboard, and grabbed a wooden spoon and rolling pin. Then she took her phone from her pocket and flicked into the Internet. 'Here we go. One historical biscuit recipe.'

It appeared to be a photograph of a page in a book. A very old printed page. 'Is that an F?' he asked, squinting at it.

'It's a long S,' she said.

'China oranges—does that say "rasp"?'

'Yes. Meaning you grate the rind,' she explained.

'OK.' He peered at the page. 'I don't know a lot about cooking, but six pounds of flour sounds a lot.'

'We'll divide the recipe by four, just to make it manageable. A pound and a half of flour, half a pound of butter, four ounces of granulated sugar—and you're lucky I'm not making you prepare loaf sugar—and enough milk to make it into a dough.'

'What's volatile?' he asked as he rolled up his sleeves.

'Ammonium bicarbonate. We'll use baking powder instead,' she said.

'OK.' He washed his hands while she took the ingredients from her store cupboards, then read the recipe again. 'Rub the butter into the flour.' He didn't have a clue what that meant, and it must've been obvious because she smiled and demonstrated. 'It needs to look like sand. Quite fine.'

Once he'd done that to her satisfaction, he grated orange rind and added it to the mixture, stirred in the sugar and baking powder, then poured in the milk and stirred it until a dough formed.

She'd already floured a marble pastry board for him.

'Is this an antique?' he asked.

'No. You get to play with the antique in a minute.'

'Seriously? I'm actually cooking with something antique? But shouldn't it be in a display case or something?'

'No. It was made to be used,' she said. 'I'd use a quarter of the dough at a time. Roll it once, turn it, and roll again.' She showed him.

'How thin?'

'Half a centimetre—or, in Regency terms, a quarter of an inch.'

He did so.

'And then you cut the dough into strips, using the rolling pin as a guide.'

'Lay the strips on top of each other in a pile to prevent the face drying,' he read.

'Don't worry too much about that. They won't dry out in the quantities we're making,' she said.

He cut the strips.

'And now for the fun bit.' She gave him a wooden block with a handle. 'This is an antique biscuit stamp, made of boxwood so it's durable and it won't taint the food.'

'Regency?'

'Regency,' she confirmed. 'Two hundred years old, so if we say each generation is twenty-five years, your five-times great-grandmother would've been a baby when this was first used.'

He handled the block reverently. The knob acting as the handle was worn smooth, but he could make out the pattern on the bottom of the block: a crown and a border of leaves. And six nails. 'What are the nails for?' he asked.

'Docking,' she said. 'The nails prick the biscuits to make sure the dough doesn't bubble up in the oven. It's old tech, but it works beautifully.'

'Like the old nursery rhyme. "Pat it and prick it and mark it with B,"' he said.

'Exactly.'

He pressed the stamp on to one of the strips of dough.

'Cut alongside the edge of the stamp, and that's your biscuit made,' she said.

It was amazing how quickly the pile of biscuits grew. And how much fun it was. Victoria transferred them to a baking tray lined with paper, and Sam realised she must have preheated the oven.

'Ten minutes,' she said. 'They would've used

wire racks, possibly lining them with paper, but we'll do it the modern way.'

Within a few moments, the kitchen was filled with a faint scent of orange.

'We dunk our biscuits in tea,' she said, 'but in Regency times you'd dip them in dessert wine at the end of a meal.'

'I can't believe you just made me bake cookies. Or that you actually use an antique in your kitchen.'

She smiled. 'I like the connection to the kitchen here from centuries ago.'

He had the strongest feeling that she used history as a protective layer. Just as he used his fast lifestyle to protect him from getting involved.

What if…?

He shook himself. OK, she wasn't like Olivia, but how did he know he could trust her?

Once the biscuits were out of the oven and cooling, she looked at him. 'So do you want me to get you a coffee of your choice from the café?'

'No. I'm happy with whatever you have here,' he said. 'As you have a modern oven, do I assume you have a modern coffee machine hidden away?'

'Using pods that will take quite a few decades to disintegrate in a landfill site?' She shook her head. 'I use a cafetière. In Regency times they

would've boiled the coffee in a pot, added isin-
glass to clarify it, then set it by the fire until
the grounds had sunk to the bottom of the pot.'

Trust her to know that.

'Have you thought about running regular
workshops here about Regency cookery? I think
you'd get a lot of takers,' he said. 'You know
your stuff. Although I'm not a cook or a history
buff, I've really enjoyed doing this.'

She went pink. 'Thanks. Maybe I should
think about it.'

'You'd be really good.'

She looked away, not quite able to accept the
compliment. From what she'd let slip earlier, he
understood why; but at the same time surely she
could see how much her parents valued her? The
only person who didn't value Victoria Hamilton, he thought, was herself.

'I'll make coffee,' she said.

By the time she'd made the coffee, the biscuits were ready and cool enough to handle. He
tried one. 'Wow. You can actually taste the orange. This is nicer than I thought it'd be.'

'I've always liked that recipe. You can tweak
it a bit to suit the circumstances—add lemon
rind instead of orange, or other spices. Cinnamon's nice at Christmas.' She fed Humphrey a
corner of a biscuit. 'You've done well.'

He'd risen to her challenge. Now it was his

turn to challenge her. 'So do I get to see these ancient recipes of yours?'

Her eyes narrowed for a moment, as if she was making a decision. 'OK. But unless your hands are scrupulously clean, I'd ask you not to touch pages of the older books—and don't touch the print. The oils on your fingers will damage it.'

'Right.' He'd put up with her being super-serious about that. This was what mattered to her—and she was sharing it with him. Trusting him. Funny how it made him feel so warm inside.

She showed him the modern edition of the medieval cookbook she'd talked about earlier. And then he discovered that some of her collection really was old. No wonder she'd been a bit wary about letting him handle it. It must be worth a fortune. He blinked at the frontispiece of one. 'That's getting on for two hundred and fifty years old. Is it from the library here?'

'No. It was my twenty-first present from Mum and Dad.'

'Most women would've asked for jewellery.'

He realised he'd spoken aloud when she shrugged. 'So I'm weird.'

'No... Just different.' And, the more time he spent with her, the more she intrigued him. Even though he'd told himself she wasn't his type, he was beginning to think that maybe she was.

Victoria Hamilton was like no other woman he'd ever met. And, if her senior room manager hadn't knocked on the door this morning, he would've kissed her.

He still wanted to kiss her. Very much. Although it also scared the hell out of him, he had a nasty feeling that, if he let her, Victoria Hamilton could really matter to him.

He distracted himself by looking at the photographs on her mantelpiece. Pictures of herself and Lizzie and their parents, as she'd expected. Her graduation. And one on graduation day, with another woman. 'Who's this?' he asked.

'Jaz. My best friend.'

The food historian, he remembered. In the photograph, Victoria was smiling and relaxed. And, for once, her hair was down. 'Are you going to wear your hair like that for the ball?'

'Regency women always had their hair up for formal occasions—usually in a bun at the back, sometimes with flowers or jewellery wound in it, and with little ringlets in the front. Which is probably how I'll do mine for the ball, though I'll use modern curling tongs rather than Regency ones.'

Trust her to know that. And she'd look beautiful.

'Right. Have you finished your coffee? The house will be open for visitors soon, and it'd be nice to give the biscuits to the stewards before we open,' she said brightly.

In other words, she wasn't comfortable with him being in her space. She was putting distance between them. Which was probably a very good idea.

CHAPTER SIX

PREDICTABLY, ALL THE stewards were thrilled by the biscuits. So were Victoria's parents. And Samuel insisted on taking samples to everyone they spoke to connected with the ball during the week, basking in all the praise.

'I could be your official biscuit-maker for the ball,' he said. 'They should go on the menu as Weatherby's Wonders.'

She groaned. 'I've created a monster.'

'Call me Frankenstein,' he said with a grin; then, before she could protest, he added, 'And yes, I know Frankenstein's the doctor, not the creature.'

'You've read it?' she asked, slightly surprised.

'No, but Jude acted in a performance,' he said. 'And he's determined that I shouldn't ever become a boring financier with no culture, so he made sure I knew the important bits.'

She couldn't help smiling at that. 'Indeed.'

'My dad,' Samuel said, breathing on his nails

and polishing them ostentatiously on his cashmere sweater, 'was so impressed with the biscuits last night that he would like to know who I am and what you've done with his son.'

She laughed. 'You're incorrigible.'

When they went to London on the following Tuesday, Jaz adored Samuel from the second he offered her a biscuit. 'It's made from a two-hundred-year-old recipe and stamped with a block that was used when my five-times greatgrandmother was a baby. *And* they're my first ever attempt at baking,' he said, fluttering his eyelashes at her.

'I'll make coffee to go with them,' Jaz said, and tried a biscuit. 'Well, now. It looks as if we might have another sous-chef to add to my third-year tutorial group,' she said with a smile. 'My second years want to know if you'll do another ball next year, Tori, so they get the same experience. My third years don't care that it's the week before Christmas and technically it's out of term-time, because they're all thrilled at having the chance to cook a historical banquet for fifty people—and even more thrilled that you're letting them stay at Chiverton.'

'I can't afford to pay them,' Victoria said, 'so the least I can do is give them a bed and their food.'

'The experience is going to be so good for them. They've all been sketching layouts and suggesting menus—even though I warned them you're probably going to use recipes from the house rather than ones from Hannah Glasse or Frederick Nutt.'

'I'm very happy to have their input,' Victoria said. 'It can be a joint thing.'

'Here you go. Six lots of suggestions,' Jaz said, handing her a file, 'and I'm pleased to say they're all original and nothing's copied from source material.'

Samuel pored over the layouts with Victoria. 'I'm assuming that's a separate layout for each course, but... I don't quite get it. They've got puddings on the table at the same time as roast meat and vegetables.'

'It's how things were served at the time. Nowadays we serve *à la russe*,' Jaz said, 'which means one course after the other. In Regency times it was *à la française*, so all the dishes were set out at the same time and you served yourself and the people round you with the dishes you wanted. Or, if what you really wanted was at the other side of the table, a footman would bring it round.'

'Right.' He still looked confused.

'Presentation was really important,' Victoria said. 'Everything needs to be symmetrical.'

'But no stream in the middle of the table with fish swimming in it, right?' he asked.

'You've obviously been talking about *that* ball,' Jaz said with a smile. 'It also has to be practical. So, right, no fish. And we're going to do this as a buffet.'

'So if you've got blancmange and jelly on the table at the same time as a game pie and vegetables,' Samuel said, 'then do people go up for a second time to make it two courses?'

'No. We start with soup and fish on a white tablecloth,' Victoria said, 'and then the table's cleared away and the next course is laid out. The tablecloths are layered over each other, so the servants can clear things away quickly.'

'A lot of the ball-goers will be Austen fans,' Jaz said. 'So you absolutely have to include white soup.'

'What's that?' Samuel asked.

'It's a sort of cream of chicken soup, made with almonds,' Victoria explained. 'Agreed, Jaz. And artichoke soup for a vegetarian option.'

'Were people vegetarian in Regency times?' Samuel looked surprised,

'Yes. They called it the Pythagorean system,' Victoria said. 'Mary Shelley was a veggie. As was her husband—and even a barbarian like you must've heard of Percy Bysshe Shelley.'

'*Ozymandias*,' he said. 'Jude used to declaim it a lot in sixth form.'

'Jude?' Jaz asked.

'Jude Lindsey. My best friend,' Samuel said.

'As in the actor?' At Samuel's nod, she said, 'I saw him in *Twelfth Night* last year and he was amazing. Usually I think Sebastian's a selfish opportunist, but your friend actually made me sympathise with him.'

'I'll tell him,' Samuel said. 'He'll be pleased.' He looked at the table plan again. 'So how much of this is vegetarian? You can't just feed them side dishes.'

'Absolutely,' Victoria said.

'What about something with tofu?' he asked. Then he wrinkled his nose. 'No, they wouldn't have had tofu in Regency England.'

'Actually, Benjamin Franklin wrote a letter from London to a friend in Philadelphia in 1770, talking about tofu,' Jaz said. 'So we could mould tofu into a fish shape, colour it with paprika, and carve cucumber scales. Call it mock salmon. We could make two smaller ones to flank the salmon centrepiece. Are we doing notes with the menu, Tori?'

'To give the historical perspective? I think we should,' Victoria said. 'And maybe include some of Victoria's recipes from her diary.'

'Two soups, salmon, mock salmon, and salads,' Jaz said.

'When everyone had finished the first course, the dishes would go back to the kitchen and the footmen would take off the white tablecloth to reveal a green one,' Victoria said to Samuel. 'What's the consensus for the second course, Jaz?'

'My students think two roast meats—chicken and beef—plus a raised game pie, with a vegetable fricassee and maccheroni for the vegetarian options,' Jaz said promptly.

'Macaroni?' Samuel blinked. 'It's not just a nineteen-fifties thing?'

'It's been about since at least the fourteenth century,' Jaz said.

'Though the Regency version would've had a béchamel sauce with lemon and nutmeg rather than cheese,' Victoria said. 'They ate cauliflower cheese, too—they called it cauliflower *à la Flamand*.'

'We can have that as a side,' Jaz said. 'My students also suggest celery stewed in broth, haricot beans *lyonnaise*, and carrots.'

'Perfect,' Victoria said. 'Maybe lentil cutlets or a mushroom pudding as another vegetarian option.'

'Done,' Jaz said, adding it to her list.

'Puddings?'

'And they're really going to be served at the same time as the mains?' Samuel asked. 'Won't they get cold?'

'Yes and yes,' Victoria said. 'We're going to cheat and use cold puddings, so it won't matter.' She looked at the file the students had put together. 'Blancmange, apple tart, lemon jelly—plus raspberry cream, because we can use one of Victoria's recipes. I'll photograph that one for you and send it over with a transcription.'

'Fantastic. So that leaves us with the sweetmeats,' Jaz said.

Samuel coughed. 'Weatherby's Wonders.'

Jaz patted his arm. 'Yes, sweetie. You can show off your biscuits. Though my students have been studying Nutt and they're dying to try out his orange, ground almond and egg white biscuits.'

'Sounds good to me,' Victoria said. 'So at this point, Samuel, the footmen take away the cloth to reveal bare wood, and dessert is laid out. Wafers, biscuits and fresh fruit.'

'Definitely including a pineapple—that would impress the guests in Regency times. You needed a hothouse to grow pineapples, meaning you'd spent a lot of money on your garden,' Jaz explained. 'And I think prawlongs.'

'That's pralines, to you,' Victoria added in a

stage whisper to Samuel. 'Almonds and pistachios browned in a sugar syrup.'

'Chocolates?' he asked hopefully.

'Anachronistic,' Victoria said. 'It'd be another forty years before dipped chocolates were produced.'

'But your modern audience will expect them.'

'No, they won't. The ball audience will be mainly history buffs. They'll *know*,' Victoria countered.

Jaz raised an eyebrow. 'This sounds like an ongoing fight.'

'It is. He wants Christmas trees and *Santa*,' Victoria said, rolling her eyes.

'You try telling a four-year-old why the mean lady in the house won't let her see Santa,' Samuel retorted.

Jaz laughed. 'You have a point. Probably with the Christmas trees as well, even though the Hamiltons weren't close to George III. But I agree with Tori over the chocolates. Best stick to fruit, wafers and sweetmeats.'

'You're ganging up on me,' Samuel complained, but he was smiling. And it was hard to take her eyes off him.

'I think that's it,' Victoria said. 'I'll make sure we have rooms ready for the students, and I'll give them a personal tour of the house. We don't usually have stuff that people can handle in the kitchen, but I'll make an exception for your students, plus I'll let them play with my collection. And I'll pick up the transport bill.'

'That'll be a minibus with me driving,' Jaz said.

'Perfect. Thanks.'

Jaz smiled at her. 'I know technically we could've done all this over the phone.'

'But it was a good excuse to come and see you,' Victoria said.

'I've managed to move a meeting so we can do lunch, if you have time?'

'Definitely.' Victoria looked at Samuel. 'Would you like to join us, or would you prefer some time to yourself?'

'How could I refuse two such charming companions?' he asked. 'Plus, as your intern, I'm supposed to be shadowing you.'

'Overqualified intern,' she corrected.

'Still your intern,' he said with a grin, nudging her. 'You don't get rid of me that easily.'

Jaz found them a table at a nearby Greek restaurant which she said served amazing *meze,* and they spent the next hour talking. When Victoria excused herself to go to the Ladies, Jaz said, 'I'll come with you.'

Victoria knew she was in for a grilling.

'Just imagine him dressed as Darcy,' Jaz said. 'You've got to do that for the promotional material for the ball. You'll sell out in *seconds.*'

'Don't say that in front of him,' Victoria begged. 'His head's big enough already. All the stewards are eating out of his hand—and even Bob the gardener has taken to dropping in to my office every morning to say hello to "his boy". Normally I have to go and find Bob for an update.'

Jaz whistled. 'Impressive. Seriously, though, Sam's adorable. I know you said you're doing each other a favour with this intern thing, but are you an item?'

Victoria felt a wave of heat spread through her. 'No. He's my intern.'

'You don't look at each other as if he's just your intern,' Jaz said thoughtfully. 'So what's the problem? He's already seeing someone?'

'No. Don't read anything into it. He's just a born flirt and a charmer, and I'm responding to that.'

'On the surface, maybe. I think there's more to him than that. Otherwise he'd be too selfish to come home and keep an eye on his parents,' Jaz pointed out.

'He's nice,' Victoria admitted. 'His dad doesn't give him enough credit. But...' She wrinkled her nose. 'I don't think he's the settling type. Plus he's already told me he thinks I'm too serious.'

'Well, you know you are,' Jaz said, giving her

a hug. 'Though he's definitely a good influence on you. It's great to see you laughing.'

Victoria ignored the compliment. 'And he's way out of my league.'

Jaz scoffed. 'Of course he isn't.'

'Come on, Jaz. The last three men who dated me saw me as the heir to Chiverton, not as me. And I was too stupid to see that they were all gold-diggers who wanted what they thought was the big stately home and tons of money.' Whereas the reality was that stately homes were massive money-pits.

'They were the stupid ones, not you,' Jaz said loyally. 'I love Chiverton, but you're worth way more than the house.'

'That's because you're my best friend. Paul made it very clear that nobody would want to date me for my own sake.' And Victoria hadn't let herself get involved since.

'Paul,' Jaz said firmly, 'was a liar and a slime-ball. He wasn't good enough for you. And I think Samuel likes you.'

'As a colleague.'

'No, I mean *like* likes.'

'He doesn't.' Victoria was really glad that she hadn't confessed to her best friend about that almost-kiss. 'Nothing's going to happen. He's negotiated some brilliant deals for me with suppliers and I won't do anything to jeopardise that. I need the fundraising to work, Jaz.'

'I know.' Jaz hugged her again. 'Make a move on him after the ball, then.'

'Maybe,' Victoria said, to stop her friend arguing. Nothing was going to happen between her and a man as gorgeous — and as unscrious— as Samuel Weatherby. They absolutely weren't suitable. Chalk and cheese. She'd be stupid to let herself hope for anything more than their business arrangement.

Jaz had a tutorial after lunch, so Samuel looked at Victoria. 'Your choice. Exhibition, museum, art gallery, or back to my flat? Jude's in rehearsal today but he'll be around this evening so you'll get to meet him then.'

'Your flat sounds good,' she said. And then, while his heart was halfway through skipping a beat, she added, 'Would you mind if I did a bit of work?'

'Sure,' he said easily. He'd pretty much expected that to be her reaction. She'd clearly enjoyed seeing Jaz, but even then she'd been focused on the task in hand, finalising the menu for the ball.

Though he'd also noticed something else. 'You said nobody ever shortened your first name,' he said. 'Jaz did.'

'I've known her for nearly ten years.'

'So she's the only one allowed to call you Tori?'

'And Lizzie.'

He frowned, remembering that she'd told him about being adopted. Had her parents been more formal and reserved with her than with their biological daughter? 'Did your parents call her Lizzie?'

'No. They called her Elizabeth,' she said. 'Which isn't to say they weren't close. Just they grew up in a more formal family atmosphere.'

'Dad only calls me Samuel when he's angry.' He looked at her. 'You always call me Samuel.'

'Not because I'm angry with you. Because I guess I'm like my parents,' she said. 'More formal.'

Except with her sister and her best friend, he thought. 'And Jaz?'

'Nobody ever calls her Jasmine. She says it's too much like "jazz hands".'

He couldn't help laughing. 'I liked her.'

'Good. Because you'll be making Weatherby's Wonders under her supervision.'

'Can't I make them under yours?'

She shook her head. 'I'm going to be running around with a clipboard and a pile of lists, making sure everything's been done.'

At his flat, he opened the front door. Funny,

he'd been away for less than a month, but he could barely remember how the place felt.

Jude had thankfully left the place tidy.

'Right. Grand tour. Bathroom—there are clean towels in the linen cupboard, so help yourself to whatever you need.' He opened the next door. 'Bedroom. Make yourself comfortable.'

'Thank you.' She placed her bag neatly in the room.

'Jude's room.' He gestured to another door. 'I think I told you he's looking after the place for me for the next couple of months.'

'So where are you sleeping?' she asked.

'The sofa.'

'But—'

'But nothing. You're my guest and my sofa's comfortable enough for me,' he cut in. 'Kitchen.'

She peered in. 'Either Jude is even tidier than I am, or this room never gets used.'

'Apart from making cups of tea and toast,' he admitted, 'it probably doesn't. Jude normally sweet-talks other people into making him dinner and he'll either pay his share of dinner or bring the wine.'

'Got you.' She tipped her head to one side. 'Though, now you know how to make Weatherby's Wonders...'

He laughed. 'I don't possess a set of scales and I'm pretty sure Jude doesn't. If it doesn't come out of a tin to serve on toast or out of a supermarket chiller cabinet to go in the micro-wave, it won't be in this room.'

'Shame,' she said, wandering over to the dining table by the window. 'You've got an amazing view here. Right over the river.'

He had a sudden vision of her in his kitchen, pottering around and creating historical dishes. A dinner party where her academic friends mingled with his City friends, where the wine was good and the conversation was even better...

He shook himself. That was *so* not happening. He didn't live here any more and he couldn't imagine anything that would make her move from Chiverton. Plus they weren't an item. He wasn't looking for a girlfriend.

'It's the same as the view from the living room,' he said, ushering her into the next room and trying to get that weird image out of his head. If he ever did settle down, it would be with someone much less earnest than Victoria Hamilton.

And he wasn't going to let himself think about what it might be like to kiss her.

She was off limits.

'This is a lovely room,' she said, walking over to the French doors in the living room. 'And you've got a balcony.'

'It's nice in the summer, sitting with a glass

of wine and watching the river,' he said. Though he was aware of how different his living room was from hers. No walls lined with books. No dog asleep on a chair. A much, much larger television with a state-of-the-art games console.

'It's lovely,' she said.

But he'd seen her apartment at Chiverton. A place that was much smaller than his but was definitely home. A living room that was practically a library, but also was a place where friends would squash up together on the sofa, or where she'd sprawl out on the sofa with a book, and Humphrey would be curled up next to her. A kitchen that was used every day, where she'd cook for friends or for her parents.

And he absolutely wasn't going to wonder if her bedroom was anything like that old-fashioned room she'd shown him in the main part of the house, with a cast-iron Victorian bedstead; or how she'd look with her hair loose and spread over her pillow...

'Do you mind if I do some work?' she asked, clearly oblivious to what was going on in his head.

'Sure. When I brought work home, I'd work on the table in the kitchen. Is that OK for you?'

'It'll be lovely, thanks.'

He didn't want her to be polite and business-like. He wanted those barriers down.

But that wasn't fair. He wasn't offering a future, and Victoria Hamilton wasn't the sort who'd live in the moment or have a fling just for fun.

'I'll make coffee,' he said. 'I'll check with Jude to see if he's going to be home for dinner. Would you rather I ordered a takeaway or would you like to go out for dinner?'

'Provided I pay, I don't mind which,' she said.

Weird how he couldn't settle to anything. Once he'd made coffee and Victoria had thanked him politely, she busied herself on her laptop. He went into the living room to give her a quiet space to work in. Flicking channels used up some time, but there wasn't anything he wanted to watch. He was bored within ten minutes of switching on the games console. Even sitting watching the river had lost its appeal.

He texted Jude, who replied that he'd be back for dinner. And then Sam lasted for as long as it took to finish his coffee before he went back to where Victoria was sitting. 'More coffee?' he asked.

'No, thanks.'

Why did he have to notice how cute her smile was?

He realised he must've been staring at her, because she tipped her head to one side. 'Sorry. Am I in your way?'

'No, of course not.'

'Something you wanted?'

Yes, but he couldn't ask. 'No.'

'Bored?'

He wrinkled his nose. 'I never used to spend enough time here to get bored.'

'In work at the crack of dawn so you were ready for the opening of trading, then out partying afterwards until late?'

Why did that suddenly sound so shallow—and, worse still, uninviting? 'Yes.'

Was that pity he saw in her eyes? 'You probably work longer hours than I do,' he said. Well, *did.* Since he'd been working at Chiverton, she'd sent him home dead on five o'clock. He'd spent more time with his parents in the last two weeks than he had in the whole of the previous year. The strain on both their faces was easing, convincing him that he was doing the right thing by moving back to Cambridge.

Today offered more proof, because he didn't feel as if he belonged here any more. He'd lived in London since his first term at university, when he was eighteen, and had loved every second of it. But he hadn't thought about the city once since being back in Cambridge. He hadn't missed it at all.

'If you're really bored and none of your friends are available,' she said, 'you could make a start on drafting the programme for our Christmas week.'

'OK,' he said. 'Mind if I sit with you?'

There was a glint of amusement in her eyes. 'We've been here before. Except your table is a bit newer than mine.'

'I guess.' Sharing his space instead of hers.

And her smile warmed him all the way through.

Predictably, Jude swept in later and charmed Victoria by wanting to know all about the house and quoting Shakespeare and Austen at her. She absolutely bloomed under his attention, still her usual earnest self but there was a sparkle about her. Sam was shocked to realise that the weird, unsettling feeling in his stomach was jealousy.

For pity's sake.

He'd never been jealous before, and he had no grounds to be jealous now. He wasn't in the market for a relationship, he had absolutely no claims on Victoria, and Jude was his best friend. Why the hell should he be jealous?

But he was.

And he didn't trust himself not to snap, particularly when Victoria—who'd refused to let him buy her dinner—accepted Jude's offer of buying them all the best pizza in London.

'Pizza's hardly Regency food,' Sam said.

'Ah, but the lady's off duty right now, so she can eat modern stuff,' Jude said with a smile.

'Plus, I hate to tell you this, but Neapolitan pizza's been around since the eighteenth century, and a kind of version of it—basically flatbread—has been around since Roman times,' Victoria added.

'Know-all,' Sam muttered, annoyed by Jude and frustrated that Victoria seemed to be blossoming so much under his best friend's attentions.

Jude and Victoria shared a glance. '"Why, he is the Prince's jester, a very dull fool; only his gift is in devising impossible slanders,"' Jude said.

'Yeah, yeah. I know. *Shakespeare*,' Sam said and scowled, even more irritated.

Jude clapped his shoulder. 'Cheer up, mate.'

'Mmm,' Sam said, knowing he was being an idiot and not having a clue how to stop himself.

'Worrying about your dad?' Victoria asked.

And now he had guilt to add to the jealousy. He hadn't even called his parents today.

This was stupid. He'd met Victoria's best friend and liked her; and he'd wanted Victoria to like Jude. The fact that she did ought to make him happy, not foul-tempered. 'I'll go and call home,' he said. 'Excuse me.'

* * *

Jude topped up Victoria's wine. 'He's not usually grumpy like this. He must be really worried about his dad.' He looked at her. 'So he's really going to stay in Cambridge?'

'You know the situation. He's doing an excellent job—obviously he's way overqualified to be my intern—and I think his dad's completely out of order with all this stuff about Samuel being reckless, because he isn't.'

'Sam parties hard,' Jude said. 'But he works harder.'

'So you've known him since university?' Victoria asked.

'Since we were toddlers,' Jude said. 'And it didn't matter that he was this maths genius and I always had my nose in Shakespeare. We understood each other.'

'He said he used to help you learn your lines.' She gave him a rueful smile. 'I'm assuming you played Petruchio at some point.'

'He quoted Petruchio at you?' Jude winced. 'I know we've only just met, but you're no Katherine. I'd say you were Beatrice, if anything.'

'Thank you for the compliment. But he might have a point.'

'So you're a Shakespeare fan?'

'*Shrew* was my A-level text. But, yes, Jaz and I used to go to all the student productions.

She saw you in *Twelfth Night*, by the way, and loved you.'

He rolled his eyes. 'Sebastian's a selfish idiot. I tried to make him decent.'

'She noticed,' Victoria said. And it occurred to her how well Jude and Jaz would get on together. Maybe she could introduce them. 'So you always wanted to act?'

Jude nodded. 'Sam bought me champagne when I got a place at RADA. Just as I bought him champagne when he got his first job—and his first promotion. Not that there was ever any doubt he'd do well.'

It was pretty clear that Jude and Sam loved each other like brothers.

'He's one of the good guys,' Victoria said. 'And he's been amazing with the restoration project. He's called in all kinds of favours I wouldn't have been able to do.'

'I think it's good for him to be out of London for a bit,' Jude said. 'And I can't believe you've got him baking.' He smiled. 'Sadly, I'm performing in the matinee and the evening show that day, or I'd so buy a ticket to the ball.'

'You're welcome at Chiverton any time,' she said. 'If you have a day off, come down and we'll cook you a trial run of some of the dishes.'

'So I get to see Sam in a pinny?' Jude grinned.

'I'll definitely give you a donation for the restoration, for that.'

'I heard that,' Sam said, walking into the room. 'If the pinny makes an appearance, there are strict rules. Very, very *strict* rules. No photographs and no video calls.'

'Spoilsport.' Jude laughed.

'How was your dad?' Victoria asked.

'Fine.'

'Good.'

Whatever dark mood he'd been in seemed to have lifted, and the conversation for the rest of the evening was much lighter. Victoria excused herself to go to bed relatively early, presuming that Sam and Jude would want some time together to catch up. But when she went to get herself a glass of water from the kitchen, half an hour later, she could hear them talking in the living room. And then she heard her name.

'I like her,' Jude said. 'And I think you do, too.'

'Don't try to matchmake,' Sam warned. 'You know I'm not looking for a relationship.'

Exactly as she'd guessed. There was no way she'd consider making a move now. She was done with making a fool of herself.

'Yes, and I know why.' Jude sighed. 'Does she know about Olivia?'

Olivia? He'd never mentioned the name before. Victoria felt sick. He'd said he didn't have a partner. Had he been lying to her?

'I haven't told her. I don't want her to know what a gullible idiot I was.'

Gullible idiot? The words were spiked with hurt. It sounded as if Olivia was his ex and she'd hurt him. Badly. Victoria knew how that felt. She'd made that mistake herself, falling for someone who had a different agenda from her own. Worse still, it had been more than once. But now she knew that her judgement in men couldn't be trusted. It sounded as if Sam felt the same way about his judgement in women. That he, too, had huge trust issues.

'Anyway, we're not dating. I'm her intern. End of.'

'That's not the way you look at her,' Jude said. 'Or the way she looks at you.'

'Still not happening,' Sam said. 'Don't interfere.'

'It's been two years,' Jude said. 'Maybe—'

'No. I don't do serious. I'm looking for fun, not for for ever.'

And then it sounded as if one of them was getting up—maybe heading for the kitchen to replenish their glasses or something. Not wanting to be caught eavesdropping, Victoria fled.

Back in her bedroom—Sam's bedroom—her mind was whirling. Who was Olivia, and what had she done to hurt Sam so much that he didn't want to get involved with anyone?

Not that she could ask him. And it was none of her business.

But it was clear to her that he didn't want to act on any attraction he might feel towards her. So she was going to have to squash any feelings she had, too, and keep things strictly business between them.

CHAPTER SEVEN

THE NEXT MORNING, Sam noticed that Victoria was very quiet over breakfast.

'Everything OK?' he asked.

'Fine, thanks.' But her smile didn't quite reach her eyes. She was quiet on the way to Mrs Prinks the costume-maker, too, whereas Sam had expected her to be lit up, talking about patterns and fabrics and design.

'So what do I need for a Regency ball outfit?' he asked.

'Breeches, shirt, cravat, waistcoat, tailcoat, white stockings, and pumps,' she said.

Nothing about colours or materials. Weird. The Victoria he knew was all about details. He tried another tack. 'I'd like to buy your dress.'

'There's no need.'

'I know, but I'd like to.' He paused. 'And then I can choose the material.'

'OK.'

What? Now he knew there was definitely

something wrong. 'The Victoria Hamilton I've got to know would've given me a lecture about authentic styles, colours and fabrics. You just told me I could deck you out in lime-green polyester with purple spots if I wanted to.'

'Sorry,' she said. 'Just a bit of a headache.'

He wasn't sure she was telling the truth. It felt as if she'd gone back into her shell. The woman who'd taught him how to make Regency biscuits and shyly tried to tease him was nowhere in evidence. And he missed her.

It wasn't until they were actually in the costume workshop and she was discussing bias cut with Mrs Prinks that the bright, sparkling academic he knew made an appearance.

'Red,' he said. 'You need a red ball gown. Bright scarlet.'

She shook her head. 'Something a bit plainer.'

'Beige?' He scoffed. 'It's your ball, Victoria. Your ballroom. And you've put a lot of work in. You should be the belle of the ball.'

'I'd rather be in the background. Red's too bright.'

'Actually he's got a point. With your colouring, it would look stunning.' Mrs Prinks took a bolt of silk from her shelf, unwrapped a few turns and held the silk up against Victoria.

The colour definitely suited her. For a moment, their gazes met, and his heart actually skipped a beat. Not good. He'd been frank with Jude last night after Victoria had gone to bed. He liked her. A lot. But he couldn't offer her for ever, he had his parents to think about, and she had Chiverton Hall to think about. He knew she was nothing like Olivia, but his ex had destroyed his trust in love.

He couldn't see how they could get over the obstacles.

There was the slightest, slightest wash of colour in her face.

'I'll take it,' she said.

Within half an hour, everything was wrapped up. They'd come back for a final fitting in a few weeks, and their costumes would be ready before the ball.

They headed back to Cambridge, grabbing a sandwich from a deli on the way to the station to eat on the train. As Sam had half expected, Victoria worked on the train. He wasn't sure if it was just her work ethic kicking in, or if she was trying to avoid him.

Just before they reached Cambridge, he sent her a text.

Have I done something to upset you? If so, I apologise, and please tell me what I've done so I don't repeat it.

She looked up from her phone. 'You're sitting opposite me, Samuel. You could've just spoken to me.'

Not when she was this remote. 'That doesn't answer my question.'

She shook her head. 'You haven't done anything. I'm just tired.'

He was still pretty sure she wasn't telling the whole truth, but he'd also worked out that Victoria Hamilton was stubborn. Pushing her now would end up with her backing further away.

He'd let it drop for today, and maybe tomorrow would be better.

'You can go straight to your parents', if you like,' Victoria said when their train pulled into the station.

'I need a quick word with Bob about the outdoor stuff,' Samuel said. 'So if you don't mind me sharing a taxi with you, I'll come back to Chiverton.'

What she really wanted was time on her own so she could get it through her thick skull once and for all that Samuel Weatherby was off limits. But he already thought he'd upset her, so she also needed to play nice—because she definitely didn't want to tell him what was going on in her head. 'Sure,' she said.

But when they got back to Chiverton, they

didn't even make it to her office before her parents intercepted them.

'Darling, did you have a nice time? How's Jaz?' Diana asked.

'Yes, thanks,' Victoria fibbed slightly, 'and Jaz is fine. She sends her love.'

'Good, good.'

Why were her parents looking so shifty? she wondered.

'You remember Donald Freeman, don't you, darling?' Patrick asked genially. 'He just popped over to say hello, so we've asked him to stay for dinner.'

Oh, no. Now she recognised that shifty look for what it was. Her parents had just found her yet another suitable man to date. They'd invited him to dinner, so then he'd feel obliged to ask Victoria out to dinner.

Maybe she really was tired, or maybe she'd gone temporarily insane, because she found herself saying, 'Well, it'll be nice for him to meet my fiancé.'

'Fiancé?' Diana stared at her in shock. 'You're engaged?'

Oh, no. Saying she was dating would've been enough. She really shouldn't have panicked and made up an engagement, of all things, but when she opened her mouth to backtrack, the lie decided to make itself that little bit more tangled.

'Yes, I know it's ridiculously fast, but you know when you meet The One, don't you, Mum?' She gave Samuel a sidelong glance.

'You mean, you and Samuel?' Patrick asked, his jaw dropping.

'Yes.' She took Samuel's hand and squeezed it, sending him a silent plea to run with this for now and she'd explain and fix things later.

'Oh, my dear boy. I'm so pleased.' Patrick took Samuel's free hand and shook it warmly.

'One thing,' Samuel said. 'This isn't common knowledge, and I need it to remain that way, but Dad's not in the best of health right now. So we weren't planning to announce anything officially until he's better.'

He was thinking on his feet faster than she was, Victoria thought. And she was so grateful that he wasn't exposing her for the liar she was.

'Of course we'll keep it to ourselves—about your father's health and about the engagement.' Diana hugged him warmly. 'I'm so sorry to hear your father's poorly, Samuel, but how lovely about you and Victoria. You know, the news might well cheer him up.'

'To be on the safe side,' Samuel said, 'I'd rather keep this between us.'

'Of course, of course,' Patrick said.

'A whirlwind romance.' Diana's face was wreathed in smiles. 'Every cloud *does* have a silver lining. If we hadn't had that problem in the ballroom, you wouldn't have needed an intern, Victoria, and you would never have met Samuel.'

'No. Just let us put our things in the office,' Victoria said brightly, not daring to look at Samuel's face. He'd sounded neutral rather than furious at the stunt she'd just pulled, and she hoped he'd hear her out and let her explain. 'We'll come up and see Donald in a moment.'

'Of course, darling.' Patrick hugged her. 'We're so pleased.'

She'd think of a way to 'break' the engagement nicely, with the minimum of hurt to her parents. But in the meantime she really needed to concentrate on the fundraising. Having to deal with her parents' matchmaking was just too much right now.

Samuel didn't say anything until they got to the office. Then he closed the door behind them. 'Right,' he said, his voice still neutral and his face completely unreadable. 'Care to tell me what that was all about?'

'Firstly, thank you for going along with it—at least for now. And I'm sorry I've dragged you into this.' She took a deep breath. 'Basically, my parents are desperate for me to find Mr Right, settle down and produce grandchildren.'

'Uh-huh.'

'Because I haven't met anyone, they've taken to parading suitable men in front of me—the sons of family friends, mainly. Donald's just one more in a long, long line. And right now I could do with not having to deal with men who don't really fancy me and are trying to be polite to my parents for their own parents' sake. I want to concentrate on the fundraising. I guess I panicked and said the first thing that came into my head to put them off—that I was already seeing someone.'

'Engaged, you said,' he corrected. 'The One.'

She squirmed. 'Again, I apologise. I panicked and they were the first words out of my mouth. I know I shouldn't have said it and I hope I haven't done any harm. You did say you weren't seeing anyone.'

'As long as your parents don't take out an ad in *The Times* or something.'

'They're not going to make any announcements without our permission,' she said. 'You heard my mum. They'll keep the news to themselves.'

'So why,' he asked, 'don't you date?'

She definitely wasn't telling him the real reason. She didn't want him to know how stupid and hopeless and worthless she was—or see any pity in his eyes when he looked at her. 'I just haven't met anyone I really want to date.'

Except Samuel himself, and he didn't count. She looked at him. 'And you don't date, either. Why not?' She held her breath. Would he tell her about the mysterious Olivia?

'I want to concentrate on supporting my parents.'

In a situation he'd only known about for a couple of weeks. What about before then? Not that she wanted to risk alienating him by asking awkward questions. She needed him to support her. Just for a little while. 'I know it's a bit of a cheek,' she said, 'but would you mind going along with this, just until after the ball?'

'Let me get this straight,' Sam said. 'You want me to pretend to be your fiancé for the next couple of months—and then you're going to break it off with me at Christmas?'

She winced. 'We might have to finesse the timing a little bit, but basically yes. It'll stop my parents trying to find me a suitable husband and give me the space to concentrate on the fundraising.'

'My parents do that every so often, too,' he said. 'They invite suitable women over for dinner parties.' It was one of the reasons he hadn't come home often enough.

'So, as you know exactly what it's like, maybe we can be each other's dating decoys?' she said.

'Lying doesn't sit well with me.' He blew out a breath. 'Going along with this means lying to your parents.'

'I know, and I feel bad about that, but it's for a good cause. And it's not a lie that will hurt them.'

'What about when we break up?' he pointed out.

'I'll think up a good reason. And I'll take the blame—I'm not going to paint you as a heartless cad or anything,' she said.

Her fake fiancé.

Then again, his last engagement had been even more fake. At least Victoria was being honest and not pretending to be in love with him, the way Olivia had. Maybe there were degrees of lying. 'What about an engagement ring?' he asked.

'We don't need one. We can say we're waiting until your dad's better.'

'And you're absolutely sure my parents aren't going to hear anything about this?'

'If we let people here know that it's a big secret, they'll all be thrilled that they've been taken into our confidence,' she said. 'And we can get them to promise to keep it secret.'

'If we're engaged, people are going to expect us to kiss.' A wave of heat spread through him at the idea. The thing he'd wanted to do almost since he'd first met her—the thing he'd almost done recently—except his common sense had held him back.

Kiss the girl.

'No, they're not. They know I'm—well, a bit formal and not demonstrative.'

'But I am,' he said. 'Maybe meeting me is what changed you. Because I'm The One.'

Her eyes narrowed. 'Are you saying you're expecting benefits?'

'I'm saying,' he said, 'that people are going to expect to catch us holding hands and kissing. Otherwise, they're not going to believe that we've had a whirlwind romance and we're engaged within a couple of weeks of first meeting.'

Her eyes widened again. 'I…'

'So,' he said. 'If I go along with this pretend fiancé thing, what's in it for me?'

'Not a reference for your dad,' she said promptly. 'I wouldn't insult you like that. You'll earn your reference.'

She might be lying about their relationship, but otherwise he knew she was scrupulously honest. 'Noted. And thank you.'

'You could,' she said, 'have a sense of doing something kind and helpful. That's what's in it for you.'

'Uh-huh.'

She sighed, as if realising that it wasn't enough. 'Or I could owe you a favour.'

'Of my choice, to be taken at a time of my choosing.'

She looked at him for a long, long while. Then she nodded. 'I forgot you're a hotshot negotiator. And I'm not in a place to argue with you right now. OK. A favour, to be taken at the time of your choosing.'

'And now we seal the deal,' he said. 'As an engaged couple would.'

Her eyes were huge and full of panic.

'It's not going to hurt, I promise,' he said, and brushed his mouth very lightly against hers. Once, twice.

'Oh! Sorry,' a voice said behind them.

'Mum!' Victoria flushed to the roots of her hair.

'I was just coming to see... Well. Come up when you're ready,' Diana said, and backed out of the office.

'Your mum's just caught me kissing you. Mission accomplished, I think,' Sam said.

'Uh-huh.' Victoria looked slightly dazed.

'Last thing. I need a pet name for you,' he said. 'I can't call you Ms Hamilton. And I'm not calling you Victoria.'

'You've only known me for a couple of weeks,' she said.

'But I'm your fiancé. Which means I get to call you a pet name.'

She shook her head. 'All my boyfriends called me Victoria.'

'A fiancé is one step closer than a boyfriend.'

'Don't push it,' she warned.

'Victoria. Vicky. Vickster. The V-woman.'

Her eyes narrowed. 'I'm no Katherine, but you could definitely be Petruchio right now.'

'Kiss me, Vicky,' he said with a grin. At her rolled eyes, he said, 'You *so* set that up.'

'Not funny.'

Just to show her that it was, he stole a kiss.

But then it suddenly wasn't funny any more, because his mouth was tingling where it touched hers.

He hadn't reacted to anyone like that since Olivia—or even with her, if he was honest. He'd asked Olivia to marry him out of a sense of duty, knowing it wasn't what he wanted but knowing he had to do the right thing.

He pulled back. Victoria's face was flushed and there was a glitter in her eyes that told him she felt this weird sensation, too.

This was *dangerous*.

'We'd better go and see your parents,' he said.

Donald Freeman turned out to be a nice enough man, but he definitely wasn't right for Victoria, Samuel thought. Thankfully, after he'd congratulated them on their engagement, he excused himself from dinner, having suddenly remembered a previous appointment. And that meant Samuel could excuse himself, too, on the grounds of wanting to check on his dad.

Victoria drove him back to his parents' place. 'Thank you,' she said.

'OK. I'll see you tomorrow. And thanks for the lift.'

'I'm doing the meal for the stewards tomorrow,' she said. 'You could ask your parents if they'd like to come.'

He sucked in a breath. 'And then yours will think they know about the engagement, and things will start to get *really* complicated. No.'

'OK. Perhaps you can take some dishes home for them, then.' She gave him a smile. 'In anachronistic plastic tubs.'

'They'll appreciate that. And I'll take some photographs for the website,' he said. 'Without any anachronistic plastic tubs in sight.'

Part of him wanted to kiss her goodnight. He'd liked the feel of her mouth against his. But that wasn't part of the rules of their fake engagement.

'See you tomorrow,' he said.

Victoria told her parents another white lie, that night: that she was tired, and could do with an early night. She sat up to make her lists of what she was going to cook tomorrow, the prep plan and the timings; but she was still wide awake at stupid o'clock, guilt weighing heavily on her. Samuel was right. When she broke the engagement, her parents would be so hurt. She should've just steeled herself and told them gently that she didn't want them to keep trying to fix her up with suitable men. It would've upset them, yes, but not nearly as much as learning the truth was going to upset them.

What an idiot she was.

She couldn't even talk this over with Jaz, because she knew what her best friend would say: that Victoria was attracted to Samuel, and her subconscious had seen this as a chance to get together with him, which was why she'd said they were engaged rather than dating.

She was horribly aware that was very near the truth. And she just hoped that Samuel hadn't worked that out for himself.

She was up at the crack of dawn and headed for the supermarket, armed with a list of groceries she needed for the trial run of the ball supper. At least she'd be so busy cooking this morning that she wouldn't have time to think. She'd left a note for Samuel, saying that she'd switched the office phone through to her mobile and was working in the café kitchen this morning; but what she hadn't expected was for him to come over to the kitchen before anyone had even started in the café that morning.

'Good morning.' She eyed him warily.

'Sous-chef reporting for duty,' he said. 'What do you need me to do? Even if it's just washing up or keeping an eye on a pot for you—you can't cook for twenty people single-handed. And I assume you're cooking with modern equipment, as you're in the kitchens here.'

'I need more oven space than I have in my flat,' she said. 'I'm sure the kitchen team won't mind giving me some help.'

'But I'm your intern. I'm meant to be helping you.'

She looked at him. 'OK. If you don't mind topping-and-tailing the French beans and peeling the carrots, that would be great.'

'Good.' He smiled at her. 'Where's Humphrey?'

'With Mum and Dad. He loves roast chicken so he's on a promise of leftovers.'

He smiled. 'And a good run, after the meal.'

'Absolutely.'

'So are we cooking the meal that you planned out with Jaz?'

'Not the whole thing,' she said. 'I'm just doing the white soup and the artichoke soup for the first course, roast chicken with roast beef, fricassee, maccheroni and vegetables for the main course, and apple tart and blancmange for pudding. I'm going to plate it up as it would've been served in Regency times, though.'

'No Weatherby's Wonders?'

She smiled. 'Everyone's already tried them and given them the seal of approval.'

'Oh.' He looked faintly disappointed, and she relented. 'OK. Make them. You're right: they'll be nice with coffee.'

'I'll make the biscuits,' he said. 'If I get stuck at any point, I'll ask you. Just tell me what else you need and I'll do it.'

'Thank you. Apart from anything else, would you mind nipping up to my kitchen and bringing the biscuit stamper down? Plus I could do with little menus being printed for everyone.'

'Sure. Talk me through what you want and I'll sort it out.'

Why did his smile make her feel weak at the knees?

Probably, she admitted to herself, because it made her think of that kiss yesterday. She'd never reacted to anyone so strongly before.

But this was just a fake engagement and she knew that Samuel wasn't really interested in her. So they'd concentrate on work. She scribbled down the recipe for him and set to work on the soup.

Samuel reappeared with the biscuit stamper and prepared the biscuits and then the vegetables. He helped her with the apple tart and the blanc-mange, and she found herself relaxing with him as the day went on, to the point where she even managed to sneak in enough time to check her emails as well as answering one important call.

She'd earmarked tables in the back room of the café, putting 'reserved' signs on them, and while the vegetables were cooking and the chicken and beef were roasting she and Samuel set the table for twenty people—the house stewards, the gardening team and the café team, plus her parents.

'This isn't quite the full menu—I'm doing more dishes with each course at the ball—but I hope you'll all enjoy this,' Victoria said when everyone was seated. 'Although I'm using period recipes, I used our kitchen here.'

'It's really nice of you to do this for us all,' Nicola said.

'Samuel helped,' Victoria said, not wanting to take all the credit. 'Even though he doesn't usually set foot in a kitchen, he did lots of the prep, and he made the biscuits to go with coffee.'

'Weatherby's Wonders,' Samuel corrected her with a smile.

She rolled her eyes at him. 'Before I bring the soup through, I have good news and bad,' she said. 'The good news is that we've got the heritage funding. Not quite as much as I asked for, but it's going to pay for three-quarters of the work.'

There was a general cheer.

'The bad news,' she said, 'is that the mould damage can't be repaired. The silk's just too fragile. We need to get modern reproductions of the hangings made, and Felicity recommends we do the whole wall. The good news is that, although the timing's tight, it should all be ready just before the ball so we'll be completely up and running.' She smiled. 'And I'd like to thank all of you in advance for your support in the Christmas week fundraising. I've got a running list of who's offered to help with what and it's really, really appreciated. Anyway. Samuel and I are bringing the soup through. We'll be serving from the table behind us. I apologise in advance for not doing this proper Regency style, with the different tablecloths and everything, but it's a trial run. There's enough for everyone to have a taste of everything, and I'd welcome any feedback because I'm using recipes from the time and they might not be to modern tastes.'

'And anything that goes down really well,' said Prue, the head of the kitchen team, 'maybe we can add to the café specials board. Maybe we can produce an historical dish once a week. I reckon the visitors would love it.'

'That,' said Victoria, 'is a brilliant idea, Prue. Let's do it.'

Samuel took photographs of the two soup tureens in situ, and then of everyone sitting at the table with their soup; and he handled the photography again when he and Victoria had set out the second course.

The food went down really well, to Victoria's relief.

And then, after coffee, Patrick stood up. 'I'd like to thank my daughter for being such a trouper,' he said. 'The amount of work she's put in is amazing. And I'd like to thank Samuel, too.'

For a nasty moment, Victoria thought that her father was going to blurt out that they were engaged. She caught her father's eye and gave the tiniest, tiniest shake of her head, enough to remind him that it was meant to be a secret. For a second, he looked crestfallen, but he recovered himself quickly. 'And thank you, all of you, for your support. We couldn't do what we do here without you.'

'Hear, hear,' Diana said, standing up to join him. 'Here's to Chiverton and the ballroom restoration.'

'Chiverton and the ballroom restoration,' everyone said, and raised their coffee cups.

Afterwards, Prue and the kitchen team insisted on helping clear away, and Victoria sent Sam back to his parents' with a pile of plastic tubs, so they, too, could taste the Regency dinner.

'He's all right, our Sam,' Prue said to Victoria. 'You picked a good one there.'

'Dad knows his father, so actually I didn't pick him as my intern. He applied, and it was convenient to give him the job,' Victoria said.

Prue smiled and patted her arm. 'That isn't what I meant. Your last young man thought he was a toff and much better than everyone else. Sam doesn't. He mucks in with all of us.'

'Sam's not my—' Victoria began, panicking.

'It's all right. I won't say anything,' Prue cut in gently. 'But I think all of us see the way you look at each other.'

Oh, no. This was starting to get out of hand. The only good thing was that her father hadn't spilled the beans about the 'engagement'. 'That was a really good idea you had about using historic dishes in the café here,' she said, hoping to distract Prue.

Prue smiled at her as if to say that she knew exactly what Victoria was doing, but to Victoria's relief Prue went along with it and talked about which recipes would work where.

When everyone had gone home, although it was dark, Victoria took Humphrey for a good run in the gardens; she practically knew the layout blindfolded but took a torch with her for safety's sake.

'I'm going to have to be really careful,' she told the dog. 'Because Samuel doesn't feel the same way about me that I'm starting to feel about him. And Dad nearly slipped up about the engagement. I'm beginning to wish I'd kept my mouth shut up and just dated Donald a couple of times to keep Mum and Dad happy.'

And in a few short weeks Sam would be out of her life and he wouldn't be back.

She couldn't let herself lose her heart to him.

This whole thing was about Chiverton and the ballroom. And that would have to be enough.

The following week saw a day that made Victoria happy and sad in equal measures: Lizzie's birthday. She tried hard to concentrate on her little sister's sweetness and how lucky she'd been to have Lizzie for thirteen years. But at the same time she was sad for all they'd missed out on. Lizzie would've been twenty-five, now. Graduated, maybe married to the love of her life.

'I miss you,' she said, arranging the paper-white scented narcissi she'd always bought Lizzie for her birthday on the grave. 'What I'd give for you to be here now. You'd love all the ball stuff. And I can just see you in a sky-blue silk gown to match your eyes. You'd be the beauty of the ball.' She blinked hard. 'I know you'll be there with me in spirit. I just wish we'd had more time together.'

Humphrey nudged her and licked away the tears that slipped down her cheeks.

'You'd love Humphrey,' Victoria said. 'And I think you'd like Samuel. I'm making such a mess of this, Lizzie. He's been kind enough to agree to keep up the fake engagement until after the ball, but I...' She blew out a breath. 'I wish I was different. That I didn't keep letting Mum and Dad down, time and time again.' She grimaced. 'Sorry. It's your birthday. I shouldn't be whinging. I love you. And I so, so wish you were here.' She stood up and patted the headstone. 'Happy birthday, darling. I'm going to make Mum and Dad our special meal tonight and we'll toast you.'

When she headed back to her office, Samuel was already there.

'Are you OK?' he asked.

Obviously her eyes must still be a bit red. 'Of course,' she fibbed.

He didn't look convinced, and disappeared, returning with two mugs of coffee and two brownies. 'In my department,' he said, 'this used to fix most things. Or at least put people in a place where the tough stuff was more manageable.'

The kindness was too much for her, and the tears spilled over.

'Sorry,' she said, wiping her eyes with the back of her hand. 'Lizzie would've been twenty-five today.'

'Ah.' He took her hand, drew her to her feet, and gave her a hug.

Part of her wanted to howl even more; part of her was really grateful for the kindness; and part of her felt an inappropriate longing to hold him back, to take comfort in holding him.

But that wasn't fair.

He was her fake fiancé, not her real one.

Too late, she realised they weren't alone. Diana was standing in the doorway,

'I take it Samuel knows what today is?' Diana asked gently.

'I do now,' Samuel said. 'A tough day for all of you.'

Tears glinted in Diana's eyes. 'Almost half her lifetime ago, the last birthday we shared.' She rested her hand on Victoria's shoulder. 'But I still have my Victoria, so I know I'm lucky.'

Victoria couldn't say a word.

'Samuel, we always have a special dinner on Elizabeth's birthday. You're very welcome to join us,' Diana offered.

'Roast chicken followed by rice pudding—her favourites,' Victoria added.

'And champagne. The last of the first case Patrick laid down, the day she was born.' There was a noticeable wobble in Diana's voice. 'We celebrate having her for those thirteen years.' She stroked Victoria's hair. 'Just as we celebrate your day, darling.'

'I know, Mum.'

'I'll be there,' Samuel said. 'Thank you for inviting me. It's an honour.'

When Diana had left, Victoria said, 'You don't have to come. I'll make an excuse for you.'

'No, I'd like to be there,' Sam said. What he wanted was to be there for Victoria and support her.

'Thanks.' She dragged in a breath. 'We don't get maudlin.'

No, they'd hide their sadness to protect each other, Sam thought.

'I'm cooking, so dinner's at my flat,' Victoria said.

'Can I bring anything? Do anything?'

'It's fine. All organised,' she said.

All the same, Sam nipped out to buy seriously good chocolates and ground coffee that had been roasted locally. He knew he'd done the right thing when Victoria hugged him spontaneously.

Weirdly, even though she was his fake fiancée, having her in his arms felt more real than when he'd held Olivia. He was going to have to be really careful not to let his feelings run away with him. She was only doing this to distract her parents until after the ball.

He discovered that Victoria had been speaking the truth. It wasn't a maudlin evening, The Hamiltons smiled and remembered the good times, and Diana had photographs on her phone. Victoria was still in the shy teenage stage, but she looked happy. And Sam found himself drawn to her that little bit more.

At the end of the evening, Victoria walked him to the gate.

'Lizzie seemed lovely,' he said.

'She was.'

He rested his hand against her cheek, just for a moment. 'I know you have survivor guilt, but you don't have to make up for her. Your parents love you just as you are.'

She swallowed hard. 'I know.'

'I don't get why you don't think you're enough,' he said softly. 'Unless it's something to do with being adopted?'

She shook her head. 'I don't have abandonment issues. My biological mother was very young when she had me. She wasn't a wild child—she'd given in to pressure from her boyfriend and she was just unlucky. Her parents were taking her away for her eighteenth birthday and I was being looked after by family friends, but the three of them were killed in a car accident. There wasn't anyone else in the family who could take me on, and my mum hadn't named my dad, so I was put up for adoption. Mum and Dad chose me.'

'And I can see how much they love you.'

She nodded. 'I've been so lucky. I've always felt loved.' She lifted a shoulder. 'As you say, survivor guilt. I think I'll always feel this way.'

'Don't. Because you're loved,' he said, 'for exactly who you are. Never forget that.'

CHAPTER EIGHT

THREE WEEKS LATER, nearly everything was organised: the plan for the outdoor lights and a special menu for the café; Father Christmas; the workshops for stained-glass ornaments, wreath-making and Christmas confectionery; and the ball itself.

The only things left to put in place were the dance music and the teacher who'd hold the workshop in the afternoon before the ball and call the dances at the ball in the evening. Michael Fillion had an appointment to come and see the ballroom that morning and discuss the ball with Victoria and Samuel.

'So have you actually done Regency dancing before?' Samuel asked her.

'Yes, when I was a student. There was a group of us who loved all the Regency stuff, Jaz included. Our dance teacher died a couple of years ago, but her daughter gave me Michael's name—he apparently took over Lily's classes.'

She looked at him. 'So I'm assuming you've never done any kind of formal dancing?'

'No.'

'Maybe Michael can take you through some steps today, if he has time.'

'Or you could teach me,' Samuel suggested.

Oh, help. She could just imagine teaching him to dance—and seeking a payment for her lessons in kisses...

She shook herself. 'I'm a bit rusty.'

When Michael arrived, she made coffee and showed him around the house, ending up at the ballroom.

'The room has perfect proportions,' Michael said. 'Did Lily ever come here?'

'Not for dancing,' Victoria said.

'Pity,' Michael said. 'She would've loved this. I like how you've got the room set up as it would've been in Regency times, with the seating by the wall. So you have a mirror over the mantelpiece, usually?'

Victoria swallowed hard. 'Yes. That's where we found the edge of the mould. The silk hangings—or at least the reproductions—will be back in place just before the ball. We've got a heritage grant to cover some of the costs, and the ball and other fundraising events that week will raise the rest.'

'It's a beautiful room. I'm glad it's being used for its proper purpose,' Michael said. 'We can have the quartet seated next to the piano—you did say your college has a quartet who'll play on the night?'

'Yes, so if you can let me know what music you want, they can rehearse.'

'Excellent. Will everyone be in Regency dress?' Michael asked.

'I think so,' Victoria said. 'If people prefer to stay in modern dress, that's fine, but I've asked that people don't wear stilettos, so the floor doesn't get damaged.'

'Very sensible. I have pumps in a selection of sizes, so my students can try out the classes in comfort and decide whether dancing's for them. I'll bring some along just in case anyone needs them on the night,' Michael said. 'And you mentioned you'd like a quick lesson now?'

'Is that a horrible cheek?' Victoria asked.

Michael laughed. 'In a room like this, it'll be a privilege and a pleasure.'

'I haven't danced for a long while, so I'm rusty,' she warned.

'It'll come back. How about you, Sam?'

'Never,' Sam said. 'I'm a total novice.'

'That's fine. I can lend you shoes. Victoria, do you have shoes?'

'In my office. I'll get them,' she said.

'Tell me your shoe size, Sam, and I'll get you a pair.'

Sam knew how much Victoria hated being in the ballroom right now, with the bare wall symbolising what she saw as her failure. 'Would you rather do this in another room?' he asked quietly when Michael had gone to fetch the shoes.

'It's fine,' she said.

He had a feeling that she was being brave about it; but if he made a fuss about it he knew it'd make her feel awkward.

Michael returned with shoes and a small portable speaker, which he connected to his phone. 'Obviously we'll have live music on the night,' he said, 'but this will do for now.'

Once Samuel had changed his shoes and the three of them had rolled the carpet back to give them a decent space for dancing, Michael talked them through the first steps. Everything was very measured and mannered, Samuel thought.

'It's a cotillion and reel,' Michael explained, 'and it's danced in sets. There might be four, eight, or sixteen of you, and you repeat the moves until each of you has danced with all the other partners in the set.'

'It's not quite what I was expecting,' Samuel

said. 'I thought it was going to be more like the ballroom stuff you see nowadays. But you don't seem to get close to each other. Even the one where we're crossing arms, my left arm's behind my back and my right arm's behind Victoria's, just as her left arm's behind my back and her right arm's behind hers. It's as much as we do to hold hands. There's no real touching. We're even standing beside each other rather than properly opposite each other.'

'It's the propriety of the day,' Victoria said. 'And don't forget the women would all be wearing gloves, so there'd be no skin involved at all.'

'Jude was saying something about the waltz being considered very fast,' Samuel said thoughtfully.

'In both senses of the word—it's very energetic as well as being considered very daring for the times,' Michael said. 'Victoria, have you ever done Regency waltzing?'

'Yes, though I'm a bit rusty,' she said.

Michael smiled. 'That's fine. Let's give Sam a demo.' He put on some music that sounded like a harp, or at the very least like the musical jewellery box Sam remembered from his childhood.

Sam watched, fascinated, as Michael and Victoria marched together, then turned to face each other, one arm above their heads like an old-fashioned ballerina pose and the other arm clasped round each other's waists, and turned in a circle. Then they lowered their arms so they were much closer and added in little hops as they spun round in faster and faster circles.

'I think,' Sam said, 'that would make people dizzy.'

'Fun, though. It's a bit like the modern quick-step in places,' Michael said. 'Come and have a go. I'll talk you through it.'

Having Victoria in his arms was dangerous, Sam thought. He was aware of how close they were; enough though by modern standards there was a lot of space between them, he could see a massive difference between the formal group dances where partners changed after every few steps and this, where you'd be dancing with the same person for the whole dance. How you were close enough to have a whispered conversation without everyone else hearing. How you could really flirt with your partner and break all the conventions.

Michael slowed the steps right down until Sam was confident, and then he grinned. 'Time to do it at full speed.'

The music only lasted for about three min-utes, but Sam could definitely feel his pulse rac-ing and felt very slightly dizzy when it stopped.

'Do you get it, now?' Michael asked.

'I think so. That was very different,' Sam said.

'It'll be even better in Regency dress,' Victoria said.

Apart from the fact that she'd be wearing gloves, putting another barrier between them. He'd enjoyed holding her hand through the dance and feeling the warmth of her skin against his.

Though this was crazy. She was his fake fiancée, not his real one—and the pretend engagement was purely to help her out and stop her parents matchmaking.

He really needed to get a grip.

The lesson was over all too soon. They rolled the carpet back to its usual position, and Michael promised to send an invoice and formal confirmation of the booking later that day. 'This is going to be a joy,' he said, shaking their hands.

Sam and Victoria went back to her office.

'Let's see where we are right now,' she said. 'OK. The workshops are sold out—I have a waiting list for people who want a place on the next ones. So maybe I should look at running the workshops once a month in future.'

'Good idea,' he said. 'How are the ball tickets doing?'

'Halfway,' she said.

'Looks as if we have a success on our hands, then.'

'Don't count your chickens just yet,' she said. 'There are a lot of things that could still go wrong.'

'Not with you in charge,' he said.

Three days later, Sam and Victoria headed for London, for their final costume fitting with Mrs Prinks. Victoria had agreed to do a guest lecture at Jaz's university on what it was like to run a stately home; Sam sat at the back of the lecture theatre and watched, spellbound, as she went through the presentation without a single note in front of her, and then encouraged questions from the students. She paid attention to what they were asking and didn't brush a single thing aside.

She was absolutely in her element, and she shone.

It would be so, so easy to fall in love with her. She was sweet, she was bright, she was enchanting. And he could even forgive the lying about the engagement, because he understood why she was doing it.

She was nothing like Olivia.

But he still couldn't quite trust anyone with his heart.

He was going to have to be really, really careful.

At Mrs Prinks's workshop, after Victoria's lecture, Sam stared at himself in the mirror when he was dressed up. He'd never been one for fancy dress, even as a child. And it felt weird to be wearing knee breeches, stockings, a frock coat and a fancy shirt and cravat. Not to mention the shoes; with their suede soles they'd be ruined as soon as they were worn outdoors in the rain. He looked like himself—but also not like himself. It was as if the centuries had just blurred.

Feeling slightly awkward, he pulled aside the curtain of the cubicle where he'd changed into his costume and walked out. At almost exactly the same time, Victoria did the same.

Sam had no idea how she'd managed to put her hair up so quickly, but she looked stunning in her red silk ball gown. Like a woman in a costume drama; and yet at the same time he could imagine her walking through Chiverton Hall, centuries ago.

'Wow,' he said. 'You look amazing.'

She blushed. 'So do you.'

'Fitzwilliam Darcy and Elizabeth Bennet, eat your hearts out,' Jaz said.

Sam swept into a deep bow. 'I hope you're going to save me a waltz on your dance card, Miss Hamilton.'

Jaz scoffed. 'Are you seriously telling me you can do a proper Regency waltz?'

He laughed. 'I've been doing homework, I'll

have you know. And in these shoes, yes, I can waltz. Miss Hamilton, if I may presume?'

Samuel gave another courtly bow, and Victoria's knees went weak.

'We don't have any music,' she mumbled, flustered.

'That's easily fixed,' Jaz said, and flicked into the Internet on her phone. 'Here we go.'

Victoria had danced a Regency waltz with Samuel before in the ballroom at Chiverton: but here, in the middle of a historical seamstress's workshop, with both of them wearing reproduction Regency clothing, it felt different. Last time, her fingers had been bare against his. Oddly, now she was wearing gloves, the dance felt more intimate. Forbidden, almost.

For a second, the workshop and Jaz and Mrs Prinks were forgotten. It was just the two of them and the music. And it would be oh, so easy to...

His pupils were huge, his green eyes almost black. So he felt it, too, that weird pull? And at the end of the dance they were only a breath away from a kiss. She felt herself leaning towards him and could see him leaning towards her; and then she was aware of the sound of applause, shocking her into pulling back.

'Very impressive. You're a quick learner, Sam,' Jaz said.

Sam bowed first to Victoria and then to Jaz. 'Save me a dance at the ball, Jaz,' he said.

She shook her head. 'I can't. I'm supervising my students.'

'Then dance with me in your serving outfit and pretend you're Cinderella,' he suggested.

'Yeah, yeah,' Jaz said, laughing.

But then she caught Victoria's gaze, and her expression said, *I'll be grilling you later.*

'You both look fabulous,' Mrs Prinks said. 'I want to take up your hem by about two centimetres, Victoria. Sam, your outfit's fine so you can take it away now.'

Sam went back into the cubicle to change out of his costume, and Victoria waited while Mrs Prinks expertly pinned the hem.

'Right. When are you going back to Cambridge?' Mrs Prinks asked.

'Our train's in an hour,' Victoria said.

'That doesn't give me enough time to do the alterations.' Mrs Prinks looked thoughtful. 'Either I can courier the dress to you, or you can come back for another fitting.'

'Or,' Samuel said, 'we can play hooky, stay overnight, come and see you first thing tomorrow for a fitting and then get the train. If that's giving you enough time to do the hem, Mrs Prinks?'

'Absolutely,' the seamstress said with a smile.

'That's settled, then,' Samuel said. 'Are you free for dinner tonight, Jaz? And maybe we can go and watch Jude treading the boards afterwards, if I can get tickets. My treat,' he said quickly, before Victoria could say a word. 'You can't argue with Mr Darcy.'

'You're not in costume any more, so you're not Darcy,' she pointed out.

He spread his hands. 'Too late.'

'Actually, that'd be really nice,' Jaz said. 'Thank you. And do I get to meet Jude?'

'I'll see what I can do. Give me a few minutes and I'll get Victoria to text you with all the details.' He smiled at Mrs Prinks. 'You've done a fantastic job. Thank you so much. I'm almost tempted to wear this tonight, except I don't want to spill anything on it or wreck the shoes—which I assume can only be worn indoors.'

'Indeed,' she said.

And, in that outfit, he'd turn every female head in the theatre, Victoria thought.

After they'd left Jaz and Mrs Prinks, Victoria said, 'We'd originally planned to go back to Cambridge, so I haven't got any spare clothes or toiletries with me.'

'My flat has a washing machine and a dryer. We can borrow everything else from Jude; or we can go shopping now, if you'd rather.' He shrugged. 'I don't think you need any make-up.'

Because she was too plain for it to make much difference, according to her ex, Paul. 'Uh-huh,' she said.

'Because you're lovely as you are,' he said softly. He stole a kiss—and then looked at her in utter shock. 'Um. Sorry.'

'It's OK. It's what a fiancé would do—even though we don't actually need to keep up the pretence right now, as my parents are nowhere around,' she said lightly, even though her heart rate had just sped up several notches and her mouth was tingling where his had brushed hers.

'Does Jaz know about the fake engagement?' he asked.

'No. Does Jude?'

'No.'

'Then we don't have to keep up the act.' Particularly as she couldn't trust herself not to fall for him. That moment in the dressmaker's had shaken her. She'd nearly kissed him in front of a very small audience that included her best friend. How crazy was that?

'OK. But staying overnight might also help to keep your parents convinced about our "engagement",' he said.

She nodded. 'I need to let them know where we are, so they don't worry.'

'Ditto,' Sam said.

Not wanting to hear the hope and happiness in her mother's voice at the idea of her staying at her fiancé's flat, when Victoria knew she was going to let all those dreams down so very shortly afterwards, she chickened out and sent a text.

Second dress fitting tomorrow, so it makes sense to stay over. Do you mind having Humphrey tonight as well? Having dinner with Jaz—she sends her love.

And of course her mother would expect a message from Victoria's fiancé.

So does Samuel. Love you xxx

The reply came back almost immediate.

H fine with us. Dying to see the dress. Have fun! LU xxx

'Everything OK?' Samuel asked.

She nodded. 'Just feeling guilty about lying to Mum.'

'The whole thing was your idea,' he reminded her.

'And not one of my better ones,' she admitted glumly.

'It's done now. Let's make the best of it.'

'Mmm,' she said awkwardly. 'I do need to buy stuff, Samuel. I can't just…' She grimaced and shook her head.

'Jude won't mind you using his shower gel or shampoo, or lending you a T-shirt for tonight. And I'll do the laundry when we get in tonight.'

'It still feels a cheek.'

He tipped his head on one side. 'Is that Victoria-speak for you want to go shopping? Because I would've guessed that unless it involved a book, something to do with Chiverton or a present for someone, you're not a shopper.'

She wrinkled her nose. No wonder Paul had called her boring. He'd even spitefully called her Vic-*bore*-ia, and the name had stuck in her head. 'That's a horribly accurate summary.'

For a nasty moment she thought she'd spoken her thoughts aloud, when Samuel said, 'Actually, that's so refreshing.'

She looked blankly at him. 'What is?'

'Being with someone who sees life as more than just buying stuff.'

'That sounds as if you've dated too many Miss Wrongs,' she said before she could stop the words.

A shadow passed across his face, and she wondered if he was thinking about Olivia. Then again, he didn't know that she sort of knew about Olivia. Not the details, just that the woman had hurt him. The more she was getting to know Samuel, the more she liked him; there was depth beneath his charm. She didn't understand why anyone would want to hurt him.

'Coffee, then. Or if you need to go and get girly face stuff, I'll stay outside the shop and try and get tickets for tonight.'

'Thanks, but I'm paying for the tickets,' she said.

'Nope. My idea, my bill,' he said firmly. 'I might let you buy me dinner, though.'

'Deal.'

By the time she'd bought toiletries and underwear, Samuel had booked tickets for Jude's play and a table for three in a nearby Italian restaurant. 'I hope you don't mind me being presumptuous,' he said.

'I'm not difficult about food, and neither's Jaz,' she said with a smile. 'What's more difficult is actually getting a table, so thank you for sorting it out.'

'Pleasure.'

She texted the details to Jaz, and they headed back to Samuel's flat.

Jude welcomed them warmly and seemed thrilled that they were going to see him perform that evening.

Dinner before the show was good, and they

spent more time laughing than talking. Jaz gave Victoria a couple of pointed looks, as if to say that Samuel was perfect for her and she really ought to act on that; but Victoria knew that this whole thing between them was fake. OK, so there had been that kiss this afternoon, and it looked as though it had shocked him as much as it had shocked her; but this was all a business arrangement. And, after her last three disastrous relationships, she knew better than to hope that this could turn into something more.

Jude was amazing and, when they went backstage to meet him and the rest of the cast, Jaz was noticeably starstruck.

'I'm so sorry that I've already got unbreakable arrangements for tonight,' Jude said, 'or I would've suggested going out. But I might see you at breakfast—and I want to see you dressed as Darcy, Sammy.'

'He looks pretty good,' Jaz said.

But Victoria knew her best friend well and her body language said, *I think you'd look even better.*

Maybe...

Back at Samuel's flat, she asked, 'Is Jude dating anyone?'

'No.' Samuel's eyes narrowed. 'Why?'

'He and Jaz seemed to hit it off. And I was thinking...'

He gave her a wry smile. 'You and I have both been victims of matchmaking.'

'This isn't the same,' she pointed out. 'We're not our parents. Plus they've actually met and liked each other. This would be a little nudge.'

'True.' He made hot chocolate and handed her a mug. 'We could pass on their mobile phone numbers and leave it to them. But you're right—they did seem to like each other.' He smiled. 'Ironic that a real relationship might come out of our fake one.'

Her heart skipped a beat. Was he talking about them?

No, of course not. He meant their best friends.

They curled up on opposite ends of his sofa, watching the river by night—the reflection of the lights and the bridges on the water—in companionable silence.

When Victoria went to bed that night, she lay awake, thinking of Samuel. The more time she spent with him, the more she liked him. But he'd made it clear to Jude that he didn't feel the same way about her, so it was pointless wishing or hoping or even dreaming that they could make their fake engagement a real relationship. It wasn't going to happen.

Sam sat watching the lights on the river, snuggled up under his spare duvet and wishing that

Victoria were still there next to him. Preferably in his arms.

He liked her. A lot. The more she came out of her shell with him, the more he was starting to wonder if maybe he could talk her into trying to make their fake engagement a real relationship. OK, so they came from different worlds, but they weren't so far apart.

Once the ball was over and the stress was off her, he'd ask.

But he was definitely looking forward to the ball. To dancing with her and seeing her shine.

Mrs Prinks was satisfied with the dress, the next day, and boxed it up for their train journey.

Outside the workshop, Victoria said quietly to Sam, 'I'm giving you the money for my dress.'

'No. I said I'd buy it for you.'

'I don't expect you to do that.'

'I'd like to,' he said. 'We're friends, aren't we?'

Her dark eyes were huge. 'I guess.'

'Well, then. Think of it as a friend doing something nice for you. An un-birthday present.'

'It feels mean and greedy, taking things from you. I'm taking advantage of you.'

How different she was from Olivia—who would've expected jewellery, shoes, and a handbag to go with the dress, and sulked if anything hadn't been expensive enough. 'Humour me,' he said. 'There aren't any strings. Or, if you really want to do something for me, you can teach me to cook something healthy but tasty for my dad.'

'I'll do that with pleasure,' she said. 'And thank you. The dress is perfect.'

Funny how her smile warmed him all the way through.

Part of Sam wished that they were at Chiverton right now, so he'd have an excuse to hold her hand. Which was crazy.

When they did get back to Chiverton, Patrick and Diana greeted them warmly—as did Humphrey, who was ecstatic at seeing Victoria again.

'I know, I know. I've neglected you for a gazillion years.' Victoria dropped to her knees and made a huge fuss of her dog.

'So do we get to see you both in your finery?' Diana asked.

'Fine by me,' Sam said. Then he had an idea. 'Meet us in the ballroom in ten minutes? We'll get changed and come straight up.'

'The ballroom,' Victoria said, grimacing, when her parents had gone.

'It's appropriate,' Sam said.

She sighed. 'I guess. OK. We'll change in my flat.'

He followed her up to her apartment. 'Where do you want me to change?'

'The living room?' she suggested. 'Knock on my bedroom door when you're ready.'

'OK.' He paused. 'Do you need a hand with the z— the fastening of your dress?'

She grinned. 'You were going to say "zip", weren't you?'

'Then I thought it might be…'

'Anachronistic. Just a tiny bit. Good call,' she finished.

He loved it when she relaxed enough to tease him.

It didn't take him long to change. Then he knocked on the door. 'Ready when you are,' he called.

She emerged, fully dressed.

'You look amazing,' he said.

'Thank you. So do you.'

He smiled at her as they walked through the house together. 'I feel as if I've just stepped back two hundred years.'

'Dressed like this, so do I.'

'Let's do what your parents expect,' he said quietly, and took her hand.

'Oh, darling,' Diana said when they entered the ballroom. 'You look…' Her voice cracked with emotion.

'You look amazing. Both of you.' Patrick said.

'I'd like to take a photograph of you both together like this.'

'Yes—for the website,' Diana agreed. 'The rest of the tickets will sell like hot cakes when people see you.'

'And we should send it with a press release to the local paper,' Sam suggested.

'I'm glad I brought my proper camera,' Patrick said. 'And if you sit at the piano, darling, and you stand this side, Samuel, I can take the shot at an angle that won't show the bare wall.'

Victoria looked totally at ease behind the piano stool. 'Do you play?' Sam asked, suddenly curious.

'She does—and very well,' Diana answered.

'Would you play something for me?' Sam asked.

'Sure. What do you want?'

'Anything.'

He'd been half expecting her to play something obscure; but he recognised the *Moonlight Sonata* instantly. 'Beethoven?'

She nodded. 'Victoria's diary talks about hearing someone play it in London.'

'It's beautiful,' he said. 'Play me some more.'

He recognised Chopin and Bach, then was totally lost when she played an incredibly fast piece.

'You're Grade Eight standard, aren't you?' he asked when she'd finished.

She gave another of those half-shrugs. 'This is a nice piano to practise on.'

Diana patted her daughter's shoulder. 'She got distinctions in all her piano exams up to Grade Eight. Our Victoria will insist on hiding her light under a bushel. And she really shouldn't.'

'Agreed,' Sam said. He took his phone out of his pocket and flicked into the piece of music he'd downloaded earlier, while Victoria was changing. 'May I have this dance, Miss Hamilton?' He pressed 'play' and bowed to her.

She went very slightly pink. 'I guess we can use that bit of the floor alongside the carpet.'

Just as they had in the dressmaker's, they waltzed together. With her in his arms, it felt as if the whole world had faded away, and there was just the two of them and the music. And it didn't matter that she'd put her gloves back on again after playing the piano; he could still feel the warmth of her skin through the silk.

When the music came to an end, it really was a wrench to stop.

'Amazing,' he said, keeping his voice low so that only she could hear him. 'You're amazing.'

Her eyes looked absolutely enormous. All he had to do was lower his mouth to hers...

He just about stopped himself kissing her stupid, the way he wanted to do. It would be in-appropriate in front of her parents. And, if he embarrassed her, he knew she'd back away from him. He wanted her closer, not further away.

'Thank you for the dance, Miss Hamilton.' He gave her a formal bow, then turned to Diana. 'Mrs Hamilton, I hope you'll save me a dance at the ball.'

'It's Diana, and it will be my pleasure,' she said. 'You both look wonderful. You'll do Chi-verton proud.'

'We will,' Sam promised. 'If you can let me have those photographs, I'll update the website and talk to my contacts at the local paper.'

'Perfect,' Patrick said, clapping him on the shoulder.

'I'll go and change back into my normal clothes,' Sam said. 'I need to keep these ones looking nice for the ball.'

'Me, too,' Victoria said.

Her parents watched them leave, smiling in-dulgently.

'OK?' Sam asked when they were back in her flat.

'Yes.'

She didn't sound OK. 'Hey. It's going to be fine,' he said. 'Everyone's rooting for you and for Chiverton.'

'Uh-huh.'

There was a sadness in her eyes, and he couldn't stop himself putting his arms round her and giving her a hug. 'I believe in you,' he said. 'You're amazing. And don't let anyone tell you otherwise.'

Oh, but they had. And it had fed into the guilt Victoria felt about being the surviving child. That she wasn't enough. That she would never be enough.

'I know you're sad about not being able to share this with Lizzie,' Samuel said. 'But maybe it's time to let the sadness go and focus on all the good memories. Maybe you can dedicate the ball and the restoration to her.'

She thought about it. 'That's a lovely idea. I'll talk to Dad.'

'You do that. I'll grab you some coffee.'

Could she let go of the sadness? Of the guilt?

It would be hard, but maybe he was right and it was time she tried.

Later that evening, Diana came to Victoria's flat.

'Everything OK, Mum?' Victoria asked.

'No,' Diana said, and enveloped her in a hug. 'Because I had no idea.'

'No idea about what?'

'That you thought it should've been you

who died and not Elizabeth. That she's the real daughter, not you.'

Victoria flinched. 'How did you…?' Then she realised. 'Samuel told you.'

'Don't be angry with him. He was just worried about you. We had a little chat.'

'And he told you.' Victoria's throat thickened.

'We *chose* you, Victoria,' Diana said gently. 'You were the light of our life. You still are. And I could never, ever choose between either of my daughters. I don't care about biology. You were ours from the second we first saw you. And we both love you so much. So very much.'

'Oh, Mum.' Victoria hugged her. 'I love you, too. And it's not anything to do with biology.'

'No. It's those dreadful men you picked. I know we should let you make your own choices and your own mistakes—you've never told me what happened and I've tried very hard not to pry—but you always seemed to pick men who didn't really see you for yourself and who didn't treat your properly. Men your father wanted to horsewhip.' She grimaced. 'That Paul—I could've horsewhipped him myself.'

'So that's why you and Dad always try to fix me up with the perfect man?'

'Not perfect, but they all had good hearts. We want you to find someone who loves you as much as we do.'

'Oh, Mum.' Guilt flooded through Victoria, and she almost told Diana the truth about Samuel, but she couldn't find the right words.

'Samuel, though—you've definitely made the right choice there. He's a keeper. I really appreciate that he told me how you'd been feeling.' Diana stroked Victoria's hair. 'Don't ever feel you're second-best. You're not. You're my eldest daughter, and I love you more than I can say. So does your father.'

'You're the best parents anyone could've wished for,' Victoria said. 'I was thinking, maybe we can dedicate the ball to Lizzie.'

'No,' Diana said. 'The ball should be dedicated to the hard-working, clever, wonderful woman who put it all together. To *you*.'

'But I…'

'You hide your light under a bushel, darling, when your father and I are desperate for you to let it shine. You have that same brightness as the woman you're named after—the Victoria Hamilton who lived here two hundred years ago,' Diana said firmly. 'Now, I want you to promise me that you won't undervalue yourself again. You're my daughter and I'm very, very proud of you. I don't just love you, I *like* the woman you've become. And every day I'm glad you're ours.'

'I love you, too, Mum,' Victoria said, wrapping her arms round Diana.

When her mother had left, she video-called Samuel.

'When did you have a chat with my mother?'

'Ah.' He looked slightly guilty. 'Interfering, I know.'

'Yes,' she said. 'But Mum and I talked about things we should've talked about a long time ago. So thank you.'

'You're not furious with me?'

'I was horrified when I realised,' she said. 'But now I'm grateful.'

'I can work with grateful.' He gave her a grin that made her feel weak at the knees, and as if this thing between them were real rather than a pretence. 'See you tomorrow.'

'Tomorrow,' she echoed.

CHAPTER NINE

THE PHOTOGRAPH MADE a whole spread in the local newspaper, along with photographs of the house.

'So are you and Victoria…?' Denise asked, looking at the photograph of Sam and Victoria together at the piano.

'We're strictly colleagues,' Sam said with a smile. That wasn't the whole truth, but he wasn't prepared to talk about it just yet. He definitely didn't want to tell his mother about the fake engagement. 'Hopefully that picture will sell the rest of the tickets to the ball.'

His mother looked faintly disappointed. 'I worry about you, Sammy. I wish—'

He cut her off by giving her a hug. 'I know, Mum, and I'm fine. Right now my priority is you and Dad—and doing a good job to help the Hamiltons.'

'I know. And I'm sure they appreciate you as much as we do,' Denise said.

Sam realised he'd definitely have to make sure that Patrick didn't bump into Alan socially for the next couple of weeks. Just in case he accidentally mentioned the 'engagement'.

'Your father and I ought to buy tickets,' Denise said ruminatively.

'Mum, that's lovely of you, but you know how much Dad would loathe dressing up in a costume and doing formal dancing,' Sam said with a smile. 'Though if you want to donate the cost of a ticket, I'm sure that would be really appreciated. And I will make cookies for you.'

'Good idea. We'll do that,' Denise said.

'Thanks. I need to go or I'll be late,' he said, and gave her another hug.

Towards the end of November, it snowed. Big, fat, fluffy flakes that settled swiftly and covered the garden in a blanket of white.

'I love this place in the snow,' Victoria said. 'It looks perfect. And it's amazing at night— with everything blanketed in snow, when you look outside it feels as bright as daylight.'

Sam looked up from the file he'd been working on. Snow. Irresistible. Would this make Victoria be less serious? 'Would the garden team mind us going out in this?'

'Provided we stay off the flowerbeds, it'll be

fine,' Victoria said. 'And you can do no wrong in Bob's eyes.'

'Then I challenge you to a snowball fight,' he said. He ruffled the fur on the top of the dog's head. 'You and me versus her, right, Humph?'

Humphrey woofed, and Sam laughed. 'That's a yes. Right. Last one out gets a forfeit.'

She grabbed her coat and they tumbled outside in a rush of laughter, pelting each other with snowballs. Humphrey bounded about between them, his tail a blur, chasing snowballs that Sam threw for him.

Sam couldn't remember the last time he'd had this much fun. 'It's years since I had a decent snowball fight. This is probably the first one since I was a student,' he said.

'It's been a while for me, too. Lizzie and I used to have snowball fights—but obviously, because she was younger than me, I always made sure I didn't throw them too hard,' Victoria said. 'And we used to make snowmen.'

'I'm up for that,' Sam said. 'And we need to make a snow dog in honour of Humphrey.'

Between them, they made a massive snowman and a rather less than perfect snow dog.

'Selfie,' Sam said, and took a snap of them together in front of the snowman, and a second snap where they'd crouched down with Humphrey. Both of them had red faces from the cold, but their eyes were sparkling.

'That was fun,' he said. 'Thanks for sharing this with me. It must've been amazing growing up here as a child, with all those trees to climb.'

'We didn't really climb trees. We used to act out being knights and ladies, with pretend sword-fights and dancing across the lawn,' Victoria said.

'Did you make snow angels?'

She smiled. 'I haven't done that in years.'

Unable to resist, Sam pulled her down into the snow. She landed on top of him, and automatically his arms closed round her to steady her.

Her face was full of panic. 'I'm too heavy.'

'No, you're not.' He brushed his mouth against hers. 'Cold snow, warm you. It's a very nice contrast.' Just to prove his point, he did it again.

This time, she kissed him back. Her mouth was sweet, and the cold and wetness seeping through his clothes didn't matter. Nothing mattered apart from the way she felt, leaning into him and kissing him.

When she broke the kiss he was shocked to realise he was shaking—and not from the cold.

'Victoria.' His voice sounded cracked and hoarse to his own ears.

Panic skittered across her expression. 'You'll be soaked. Freezing. We'd better go in.'

He didn't want to move, not when she was in his arms. 'I'm fine.' He stroked her hair.

'You're cold. And wet. I don't have anything that would fit you, but I'm sure Dad can lend you some dry clothes.'

She was babbling, and they both knew it.

If he pushed her now, she'd really panic. Whoever she'd last dated had obviously really hurt her—and Sam, who'd never thought of himself as the violent type, found his fists actually clenching with the urge to punch the guy.

He let her climb off him and lead the way back to the house.

'Go up to my flat and have a hot shower,' she said. 'I'll bring you something of Dad's, and if you leave your wet stuff outside the bathroom door I'll put it in the tumble dryer.'

'Thanks.' He looked at her. 'You're as wet as I am. You have a shower and change first, and I'll make us both a coffee—if you don't mind me using your kitchen.'

'OK. Thanks.'

What had she been thinking?

Well, obviously she *hadn't* been thinking. She'd lost herself in old memories of snowball fights and making snowmen, enjoying herself with Samuel.

That kiss… It had been propinquity, that was all. Victoria knew Samuel didn't want a proper relationship. They were becoming friends, but the kiss hadn't meant anything to him, and she would be stupid to let it mean anything to her.

She showered and changed. 'Back in a tick. I've left you clean towels,' she said, not meeting his eyes.

'Thanks. I've left your mug of coffee by the kettle.'

'Great. I appreciate that.' She borrowed some dry clothes from her dad, then rapped on the bathroom door. 'The dry clothes are outside the door,' she called. 'See you back in the office.' And she fled before she could make more of a fool of herself.

When Samuel came down to her office, a few minutes later, Victoria's vision blurred for a second. She could imagine him leaning against their shared desk in forty years' time, laughing and with a mug of coffee in his hand. Just like her father had shared this office with her mother. And it put a lump in her throat.

But it was pointless wishing for something she couldn't have. Samuel had broken down some of her own barriers, but his were still in place. Whatever he'd said about her being enough, he'd meant enough for her parents—not for him.

'I put your clothes in my dryer,' she said. 'Give it half an hour and I'll go and check if they're ready.'

'Thanks. And it's kind of your dad to lend me stuff.'

'No problem,' she said lightly.

'I guess our snow break's officially over.'

He looked slightly wistful. Was it the snow he was thinking about—or when he'd kissed her?

She shook herself. Not appropriate. 'It is. And I have a pile of stuff to do.'

'We'll divvy it up between us,' he said.

Sam stuck to being professional with Victoria for the next couple of weeks. But, the week before the Christmas events, he sat on the edge of their shared desk. 'Engaged couples go out to dinner. Or dancing.'

She frowned. 'We've done dancing.'

'Regency dancing,' he said. 'Not modern.'

She spread her hands. 'Can you imagine me in a nightclub?'

'Well—no,' he admitted. 'But your parents are going to start wondering why we're not going out anywhere on dates.'

'They can see we're really busy with the

Christmas week preparations,' she pointed out. 'The house opens on Sunday.'

'We could,' he said, 'have a night out in London. There's a performance I thought it'd be fun to go to.'

Her eyes widened. 'Are you asking me out on a date?'

'A fake one,' he said quickly, not wanting to spook her.

'OK.'

'Friday night?' And maybe he could talk Jude into staying at a friend's for that night. 'Everything's on track and we'll be back for Saturday afternoon to deal with any last-minute troubleshooting. Plus I think it'll do you good to take an evening off—before you burn out.'

For a moment, he thought he'd pushed her too far; but then she nodded.

'You're right. And thank you—that'd be nice to go to a show.'

On Friday, they dropped their things at Samuel's flat and went for an early dinner. When they walked to the theatre, the show name was in lights outside: *The Taming of the Shrew.*

'Really?' she asked. Did he still think she was a shrew?

'Sorry, I just couldn't resist it,' he said with a grin. 'But we do have good seats.'

'It's a while since I've seen it. And Shakespeare's always a treat.'

'"Why, there's a wench. Come on and kiss me—Vicky."'

He pronounced the 'ky' as 'Kate' and she groaned. 'That's terrible.' But she couldn't help smiling.

They walked into the foyer, and suddenly he grabbed her hand.

'What?' she asked.

'That favour? I'm calling it in, right here and right now,' he said. 'Can you please just go with whatever I say next?'

She'd done that to him without any prior warning, and he'd gone along with her; the least she could do was agree now. 'Sure.'

'You can start by kissing me. Not full-on snogging, just kind of stealing a kiss. Like a fiancée would.'

She had absolutely no idea what had spooked him like this, but she could see the wariness in his eyes. Something was definitely wrong. 'Well, sweetie,' she said softly, resting her palm lightly against his cheek. 'Let's do this.'

She reached up and brushed her mouth against his and he wrapped his arms round her, holding her tightly as if she were the only thing stopping him from drowning.

'Thank you,' he whispered against her mouth.

'Sam? Sam Weatherby? I *thought* it was you!' a voice cooed behind them.

'Olivia,' he said coolly.

Olivia? *The* Olivia? Victoria wondered.

The woman who was sashaying over to them with a man in tow was tall and willowy, with immaculate blonde hair and the kind of high-maintenance barely-there make-up that took an hour to do. Her clothes were all clearly designer labels, Victoria would bet that her shoes cost a fortune, and Olivia was wearing enough jewellery to dazzle the entire theatre.

'Good to see you, Sam.'

From the look in his eyes, Samuel didn't think it was good to see her—or maybe it was her companion that he objected to. But he said politely, 'And you.' Though Victoria noticed that his eyes didn't crinkle at the corners when he smiled.

'This is Geoff, my fiancé,' she said. 'Darling, Sam and I are old friends.'

That wasn't quite how Victoria would describe it. That snippet of conversation she'd overheard between Samuel and Jude had told her that Olivia and Samuel had been a lot more than friends. And that it had gone badly wrong.

'Good to meet you, Geoff,' Samuel said, shaking the other man's hand. 'And may I present my fiancée, the Hon Victoria Hamilton of Chiverton Hall.'

Now Victoria realised what his favour was: the same as she'd asked of him. Except she was distracting his ex rather than his parents.

Though she didn't have time to wonder if it meant that he was still in love with Olivia, because she'd promised to go along with what he asked.

'Goodness! I didn't realise you'd got engaged.' Olivia's expression was very put out for a moment; then she looked Victoria up and down. Her gaze settled on Victoria's bare left hand, and then she made very sure to clutch her own left hand—which had the most massive diamond on her ring finger—to her chest, to accentuate the difference between them. She gave Victoria a slightly triumphant smile, as if to say that in no way could she imagine someone as attractive as her ex-fiancé wanting to settle down with someone who just wasn't pretty enough or scrubbed up well enough to compete with Olivia herself. 'Well, I do wish you the best. I take it your ring's being resized at the moment? Or is he making you wait, Vicky?'

'My name is Victoria, not Vicky,' Victoria corrected coolly. 'And, actually, we're not bothering with a ring, Lily.' She deliberately got the other woman's name wrong, and she could see that the barb had hit home. 'Real love doesn't need the trappings and suits.' Before the other woman could make a spiteful comment, she linked her fingers through Sam's. '"My bounty is as boundless as the sea, My love as deep; the more I give to thee, The more I have, for both are infinite."' She drew Sam's hand up to her mouth and kissed the backs of his fingers. 'Which obviously is Juliet rather than Katherine, but what's a play between people who love each other?'

Olivia's expression was like thunder.

'So nice to meet you, Lily,' Victoria said, letting just a hint of patronisation into her tone. 'But I think we're being called to our seats right now. Enjoy the play.' She tugged at Sam's hand, and headed towards one of the doors. 'If this is the wrong way to our seat, it doesn't matter. We'll find another way round,' she said out of the side of her mouth.

Sam took their tickets out of his pocket. 'This is the right door, and hopefully they're not sitting anywhere near us.'

She hoped so, too. 'Are you OK?' she asked, seeing the tension in his eyes.

'Yes.' That was a lie, she knew. 'And thank you for coming to my rescue.'

'No problem.' She squeezed his hand, letting him know she was firmly on his side. If that woman thought she was going to get a second chance to hurt Samuel, she had another think coming. 'She's a festering lily.'

Samuel looked at her. 'That's Shakespeare, right?'

'Sonnet Ninety-four.' In the looks department, Victoria might be a base weed, but Olivia was most definitely a festering lily, and Victoria knew which of the two she'd rather be. 'Ask Jude.'

'Is that why you called her Lily instead of Olivia?'

'I was being petty,' she admitted. 'But it turned out to be appropriate.'

'Yeah.'

To Victoria's surprise, Samuel didn't let her hand go. He held it throughout the whole play, and all the way back to his flat. She didn't comment on it or push him to talk until they had arrived.

'Coffee, wine, or something stronger?' she asked.

'I'm fine.'

'No, you're not.' She gave him a hug. 'Look, I know it's not really any of my business, but seeing Olivia clearly threw you. I'm assuming she's your ex.' She knew that for sure but didn't want to admit to eavesdropping. And he'd helped her overcome feeling as if she was worthless. The least she could do was to be there for him. 'I'm here if you want to talk.'

'I don't really want to talk,' he said, 'but I owe you an explanation.'

'You don't have to tell me anything if you don't want to,' she said.

She thought he was going to close up on her, but then he sighed. 'Olivia was my fiancée.'

Now she understood why Samuel had wanted her to pose as his fiancée tonight. She had a feeling that the whole flashing-my-massive-diamond thing had been Olivia's way of telling him that she'd met someone who suited her better.

'We met at a party, a friend of a friend kind of thing, and…' He grimaced. 'Let's just say I wasn't very nice when I was in my early twenties. I dated a lot. I never, ever cheated on any of my girlfriends, but I never really gave any of them a chance to get close to me, either. I didn't let the relationship develop into anything deeper because I thought the world was my oyster and I had all the time in the world—or maybe my dad was right in that I was selfish and reckless and thoughtless. But somehow Olivia stuck. We'd been dating for six months when she told me she was pregnant.'

Victoria waited.

'So I did the right thing. I didn't think I was really ready to settle down—but she was my girlfriend and she was pregnant with my baby, so of course I wasn't going to abandon her. I asked her to marry me. She said yes.' He closed his eyes for a moment. 'It was only when I accidentally saw a text on her phone—it was on the lock screen,' he added quickly. 'I wasn't snooping. I just glanced casually at the screen when the light came on, as most people do, and I saw the words. It was from one of her friends. She seemed to be laughing at the fact that Olivia had pulled it off.'

Victoria frowned. 'Pulled what off?'

'The trap she'd set for me,' Samuel said. 'The massive rock on her finger, moving into a flat overlooking the river—not this one, I moved here later—and the fact she was never going to have to work again. Because that's what it was, a trap. She wasn't actually pregnant. She just knew that was what it would take for me to marry her—and, once she was married to me, that would mean either sticking with it or handing over an expensive divorce settlement.'

Victoria blinked, not quite taking it in. Olivia had pretended she was pregnant, just to make sure Samuel married her and financed her lifestyle? 'That's a horrible thing to do. What about love?'

'That's when I realised Olivia loved only herself,' he said dryly. 'And she made sure we both saw tonight how massive her new engagement ring is. Bigger than the last one. I feel sorry for the guy, because I don't think she's capable of loving anyone.'

Now Victoria understood that conversation she'd overheard. Why Samuel felt he'd been naive and gullible. But he hadn't. He'd been *decent*. 'So what happened? Did you confront her with the text?'

'I lied. I said I'd overheard her talking to her friend Hermione about the baby that didn't exist and suggested that she might like to tell me the truth. I thought she was going to tough it out, but then she crumpled and admitted it. And I ended the engagement right there and then. I gave her a month to find somewhere else to live and I moved in with Jude. I followed up with a letter from my solicitor, and I think she realised she wasn't going to get anything else out of me—so, thankfully, she left. She stripped the flat, but she left.'

No wonder he had trust issues. Olivia had treated him even more badly than Paul had treated her. 'I'm sorry. That's a horrible thing to happen.' She frowned. 'Though, as she was supposed to be pregnant, um, didn't you notice?'

'That she was still having periods? No. Hers were never regular, and her boss sent her on a couple of courses. I realised later the timing of the "courses" must've coincided with her periods. I wouldn't be surprised if she'd just taken time off and was staying with Hermione rather than going away somewhere on a real course.' He lifted a shoulder. 'I was a gullible, naive fool.'

'No, you weren't. You did your best by her,' she said. 'And we all want to be loved. It's easy to convince yourself someone loves you; it's really not very nice to realise that actually they're looking at your assets instead.'

'That,' he said, 'sounds personal.'

She inclined her head. 'Stately homes are worth a lot of money. But, unless you've grown up with one or worked in one, you might not realise that owning a stately home means you're asset-rich and cash-poor. Or that stately homes cost an awful lot of money to run.'

'You had a guy like Olivia?' he asked.

'Yes, but we didn't get as far as an engagement, and unlike you it took me three attempts before I finally twigged why any of them wanted to date me.' She grimaced. 'I'm a slow learner. The last guy made it very clear to me that the house is the only attractive thing about me.'

'You,' he said, 'are far from being a slow learner. Your mind's first-class. And words fail me about your ex. That's a vile thing to say, and it's not true.'

She shrugged. 'I saw the way Olivia looked at me tonight. With pity. I'm not like the women in her world—well, in your real world. I don't have an expensive hairdo, expensive shoes, expensive clothes, expensive make-up or expensive jewellery.' She didn't want them, either. They weren't important.

'You don't need them.'

'Thank you for being gallant, but I'm not fishing for compliments. I'm aware of what I am.'

'I don't think you are,' he said. 'When you're talking about history, you light up. And that's *my* Victoria. The one who pays attention to detail, the one who knows obscure stuff and delights in it.' He smiled. 'The one who doesn't bat an eyelid when her muddy dog puts a paw on her knee. Yes, you can be horribly earnest and over-serious, but there's a warmth about you and you've got a huge, huge heart: and that's what I see. It's like that thing you were saying to Olivia about trappings and suits—you don't need them. You're enough as you are. Not just for your parents. For *anyone*.'

Tears pricked at her eyelids and she blinked them back. 'That's such a nice thing to say.'

'I'm not being nice. I'm being honest.' He wrapped his arms round her. 'I happen to *like* you.'

Her throat felt thick. 'I like you, too.'

'I mean I really, *really* like you.' He stole a kiss. 'And this is nothing to do with Olivia and everything to do with you.'

This time, when he bent his head to kiss her, she kissed him back. And she made no protest when he picked her up and carried her to his bed.

The next morning, Victoria woke in Samuel's arms. She was pretty sure he was awake—his breathing wasn't deep or regular—and she didn't have a clue what to say to him. This was so far outside the way she usually behaved. She had no idea of the protocols. Had this been a one-night stand, or was it the start of something else?

She still didn't have her thoughts clearly together when Samuel said softly, 'Good morning.'

'Um. Good morning.' She wanted to bury her head rather than face him, but the way she was lying meant that would mean burying her head in his bare chest. And she didn't want him thinking she was needy or would make any kinds of demands on him.

'Are you OK?' he asked.

This time, she met his gaze. 'Yes.' She wasn't—she was all over the place—but no way was she admitting that. 'Are you?'

'Yes and no.' He shifted to kiss the tip of her nose. 'I'm better for waking up with you in my arms.'

'Uh-huh,' she said, not knowing what he wanted to hear.

'Last night probably shouldn't have happened—but I'm glad it did.'

So was she. Though part of her felt antsy. She was used to everything being under control and ticked off a list. This was stepping so far away from that, it sent waves of panic through her. 'So where do we go from here?' she asked.

'I don't know,' he said. 'Maybe see how things go. Though obviously we have next week to get through, first.'

And then his internship would officially be over. 'Then you'll be busy taking over from your dad.'

'But,' he said, 'at least we'll be living near each other. And maybe we can...' He blew out a breath. 'I'm not very good at proper relationships.'

'Neither am I,' she admitted.

'Then maybe we can learn together,' he said. 'Learn to trust each other, learn to make it work.'

Was she hearing things?

'If you'd like to, that is,' he added.

He meant it. He really meant it. And her heart felt as if it would burst with joy. 'I'd like that. A lot,' she said.

He kissed her again, and by the time they got

up it was way too late for breakfast. Especially as they had a train to catch.

'Maybe we should have brunch on the train while we go through our lists?' he suggested.

'Good idea.'

Even though they were officially going through all the things they needed to troubleshoot before the house opened to visitors the following afternoon, Sam found himself distracted by Victoria on the train. There was a new softness to her expression when she looked at him. And the way she made him feel... It was a long time since he could remember being this happy. This thing between them was new and fragile, but he knew she was Olivia's opposite—she was honest and fair and *nice*.

When they reached Cambridge, he took his phone from his pocket to call them a taxi. Then he realised that he must've left his phone switched on silent from the theatre, the previous night, because there were five missed calls from his mother, and a text.

Please call me urgently, Sammy.

He felt sick. Had something happened to his dad? 'I need to call my mum,' he said to Victoria. 'Anything I can do?' she asked.

He shook his head and called his mother.

'Sammy, we're at the hospital. Your father had a stroke this morning,' Denise said.

'I'm on my way,' he said. 'I'm at the station. I'll get a taxi straight to the hospital. Text me the ward name and I'll text you when I'm nearly there.'

'Samuel? What's happened?' Victoria asked when he ended the call.

'Dad's had a stroke. I need to get to the hospital.'

'I'll come with you.'

To the hospital?

Given that she'd lost her sister to leukaemia, Sam was pretty sure that Victoria would find hospitals difficult. In her shoes, he would. OK, so she'd offered to go with him—but it wouldn't be fair to take her up on that offer.

Right now he had no idea what the situation was with his dad. The stroke might've been mild, it might've been severe, or it might've been the first of a series that would end in Alan's death. He couldn't hurt Victoria by making her face that.

He shook his head. 'You have things to do at the house.'

'They can wait.'

He dragged in a breath. 'I need to do this on my own.'

'Anything you need, just call me. *Anything,*' she said. 'It doesn't matter how big or small, or what time it is. Call me.'

Right now what he really wanted was to turn the clock back and for his dad to be OK. But that wasn't possible. 'Thanks,' he said. 'I'll call you later.'

'Give my best to your parents.'

'Thanks. I will.'

The drive in the taxi felt as if it were taking for ever. Seeing his father in a hospital bed, with Alan's mouth twisted and one eye half shut, was a shock.

'Mum. I'm so sorry.' He hugged his mother, and sat on the edge of his father's bed, taking Alan's hand. When had his father's skin become this papery—this *old*? 'Dad, I'm here. I'm sorry.'

The sounds that came out of his father's mouth didn't bear much resemblance to words.

'Don't try to talk. Just rest. I'm here now,' Sam said.

Time, at the hospital, was different. Like treacle. And, although the medical staff were kind, nobody could give any real answers about when—or if—Alan would recover his powers of speech or walk again. Sam was used to organising things, making things happen; the seven words he kept hearing drove him insane. *We'll just have to wait and see.*

How long would they have to wait?

And actually having to feed his father because Alan couldn't hold cutlery or a cup or a sandwich. Sam knew how much his father was hating this. The loss of control. The loss of his dignity.

All Sam could do was to grit his teeth and hold both his parents' hands. 'We'll get through this,' he said. 'We'll get you back on your feet and back to your normal self, Dad.'

His phone beeped several times but he ignored it, until Denise pushed him to go and get himself a mug of coffee. Then he checked his messages.

There were a couple from Victoria. Not demanding, needy, look-at-me messages like the ones Olivia had been fond of sending. Just a quiet, At Chiverton. Hope your dad's doing OK. Thinking of you all.

There wasn't much he could say to that. Because right now nobody knew how his dad was doing.

Thanks, he typed back.

He wished he hadn't pushed her away and told her to go back to Chiverton. Right now he could really do with her arms round him, His steady, quiet, *safe* Victoria.

But that wasn't fair.

Hadn't his father said he was selfish and reckless?

There was a second text, sent two hours later.

Let me know if there's anything I can do. Any time.

She was so kind and supportive: and, at the same time, it was clear she was trying to give him space and not pressure him. That she understood what it was like to be at the bedside of someone you loved, worried sick, and she wouldn't be huffy if he didn't reply within a couple of hours, let alone within seconds.

And because he knew what she'd been through, he knew he had to do the right thing. Distance himself. Protect her from having to face this nightmare all over again. So, later that evening, he sent her a text.

Sorry to let you down. I need to support my parents right now. Book a temp to help you next week and I'll pick up the bill. Hope all goes well with the ball.

Victoria stared at the text.

He'd said nothing about how his dad was. How *he* was. He'd ignored the supportive texts she'd sent him—and she hadn't flooded his phone with needy messages, either. She'd simply told him when she got back to Chiverton and asked him to let her know if there was anything she could do. She'd tried to be supportive and give him space at the same time.

She blew out a breath and tried to unpick his message.

Sorry to let you down.

Of course he wasn't letting her down. This was an emergency.

I need to support my parents right now.

Again, in his shoes, she'd feel the same. It wasn't a problem.

Book a temp to help you next week and I'll pick up the bill.

Meaning that he wasn't coming back as her intern. It would be a bit of a headache for her, but over the weeks she'd worked with him she'd discovered that they had the same attitude towards project management and she knew his files would contain all the information she'd need to keep everything ticking over. As for getting in someone to help her—she'd just pick up the slack herself. She didn't expect him to pay for a temp to replace his unpaid position.

Hope all goes well with the ball.

And that was the bit that stuck in her throat. He wasn't coming to the ball. She'd so been looking forward to it. To dancing with him in the restored room, dressed up in her Regency finery.

OK. She'd have to stop being selfish and suck it up. Samuel's dad was seriously ill. Of course he wouldn't want to come and do something so frivolous.

She had no idea whether his phone was even on, so a text was the easiest way to reach him. He'd pick it up whenever.

You're not letting me down and of course I understand your parents need you. Let me know if there's anything I can do.

She didn't quite dare add a kiss. Because now she was starting to think that what he'd said to her in London had been in the heat of the moment.

You're enough as you are. Not just for your parents. For anyone.

Maybe he'd meant it at the time. But now all her old fears came flooding back. She hadn't been enough for Paul, and Samuel was ten times the man Paul was. Whatever made her think she'd be enough for him?

And how selfish was she, putting her own feelings first when she knew how ill his father was?

She'd do what he wanted and keep her distance.

Victoria was nothing like Olivia. Of course she'd be understanding and wouldn't put pressure on him, Sam thought. She was kind. She offered help because she genuinely cared and wanted to help, not because she thought it would score points.

But everything was muddled in his head. Right now he couldn't get over the fact that his father was seriously ill.

Alan Weatherby had definitely got the measure of his son. Reckless and selfish.

So maybe it was time to be unselfish and not keep Victoria dangling on the hook. She had enough on her plate without worrying about him.

He'd do what he always did with relationships. Distance himself.

Thanks, but no need. Good luck with the future.

CHAPTER TEN

GOOD LUCK WITH the future.

That sounded pretty final, Victoria thought.

Obviously Samuel didn't plan to be part of that future.

What an idiot she was. So much for thinking she'd learned her lesson. Yet again she'd fallen in love with a charmer who didn't feel the same way about her. Though at least Samuel hadn't had his eye on the house.

She'd just have to suck it up and deal with it. The only thing she could do was to visit Alan Weatherby in hospital when he was a little better and give Samuel the glowing reference he deserved. Just because things hadn't worked out between them, she wasn't petty enough to deny the hard work he'd put in.

In the meantime, she had enough to keep her super-busy, with the house due to open for visitors, the workshops and the ball.

She spent the day putting the finishing touches

to the Christmas trees and trying not to think about how she and Samuel had collected the pine cones and the giant allium heads together and spray-painted them gold. She made a couple of kissing balls, binding the hoops together with string and covering them with greenery, adding dried orange slices and ribbons and mistletoe; and all the while she tried not to think about kissing Samuel. She made pomanders, pressing cloves into oranges and tying them with ribbons. Having something to do that required her attention so she didn't have time to think was really, really good.

The team who always did her flowers had gathered greenery to be spread along the windowsills and mantelpieces, and they'd done her proud with the table centrepieces.

And the one good thing about working ridiculous hours was that it meant she was physically so tired that she actually slept instead of lying awake, brooding.

The next day, Samuel's team of footmen and servants turned up—thankfully in exactly the kind of clothes they would've worn in Regency times. She set them to work with Nicola, sorted out a room for her anachronistic Santa, and made sure she was around in case any of the visitors had any questions.

Despite the fact that all their visitors seemed delighted to have the chance to talk about Regency Christmas customs and she was rushed off her feet, she still missed Samuel. Every so often she found herself turning to say something to him—and of course he wasn't there.

Stupid, stupid, stupid.

Once the house had closed, she cut some flowers from the garden, then headed for the hospital.

'Sorry, we don't allow flowers at the moment,' the receptionist on the ward told her. 'We have strict rules for controlling the spread of infection.'

'Of course. Sorry.' She bit her lip.

But at least they allowed her to visit Samuel's father. And, thankfully, Samuel wasn't there.

'Mr Weatherby? I'm Victoria Hamilton—Patrick and Diana's daughter,' she said. 'I did bring you some flowers from Chiverton, but unfortunately I'm not allowed to give them to you.'

'Thank you anyway.' Alan squinted at her.

'I'm so sorry you're ill.'

'Getting better. Words aren't…' He grimaced. 'Can't get the right ones.'

'They'll come back,' she said, wanting to reassure him.

'Got some words today, though. Getting better. You work with Sammy.'

She nodded. 'Your son is a good man. He's

way overqualified to be my intern, but he did the job anyway, with a good heart. He's easy to work with.'

Alan frowned. 'Reckless.'

'A little bit headstrong at times,' she said, 'but Samuel listens to people. He thinks about things. He's impulsive, yes, but that's not a bad thing because he has great ideas.'

'You taught him to bake.' Alan smiled. 'His mum nearly fell over.'

She smiled back. 'He was very pleased with himself about that. And he insisted on making everyone in the house try the biscuits. He's— *was*,' she corrected herself, 'going to make them for the ball. They're on the menu as Weatherby's Wonders.'

'Weatherby's Wonders.' Alan gave a wheezy chuckle.

'Mr Weatherby? Are you all right? Can I get you a glass of water, or would you like me to call a nurse?'

'I'm all right, love.' He patted her hand. 'Tell me. Sammy.'

There was a lot she could say about Samuel, but it wasn't appropriate. Instead, she said, 'He's kind to my dog, he makes time for everyone on the team and makes them feel valued, and our head gardener Bob—who's notorious for being grumpy—has taken a real shine to him and comes into the office for a daily cuppa with him. I miss him. We *all* miss him,' she added swiftly.

'You think he could take over?'

'From you? Yes. No hesitation. Samuel would make an excellent job of anything he decided to do.'

'You'll give him a...?' Alan frowned, clearly unable to find the right word.

'Reference?' She nodded. 'He's more than earned it. He's done everything from spray-painting pine cones, to organising a Santa and negotiating an amazing deal on Christmas trees. He learned to bake from a recipe that's centuries old, and he learned the steps to the Regency dances when he'd never done anything like that before. He never complained once. Argued with me, yes, but he had valid points.' And he'd stolen her heart in the process.

Samuel recognised that voice.

He stopped dead, not wanting Victoria to see him. What was she doing here?

Knowing that he shouldn't be eavesdropping, he listened.

She was talking to his father. And she was really giving him a glowing report.

Guilt flooded through him. He'd pushed her away—and she'd still come to give support, in a place that had to be difficult for her. She could've just ignored all this or sent a formal letter with a reference, especially as she was right in the middle of the fundraising and she was horrendously busy.

But she hadn't. She was here in person. Not to score points, but because Victoria Hamilton was a really, really good woman. Dependable. Trustworthy. Brave.

I miss him.

Yeah. He missed her, too. So much that it actually hurt. But he didn't know what to say to her; and all the things that were in his head definitely weren't appropriate to say in front of his father. Plus he didn't want to do anything that might make his father have a relapse or a second stroke.

This was a conversation he needed to have with Victoria, on his own—and not right now. For his father's sake, he'd go and have a cup of coffee and come back in half an hour.

As for Victoria herself… He was going to have to sort that out, too. He'd let her down. Hurt her. He wasn't entirely sure how to fix it, but he'd find a way to make a start. Because hearing her voice again had crystallised everything for him. He finally knew what he wanted for the rest of his life. The question was whether she wanted that, too. But the way she spoke to his father gave him hope.

* * *

The workshops went brilliantly, including the pre-ball dance workshop. Victoria had to nip out to the supermarket and get emergency supplies for the café, because they had even more visitors than she was expecting. The reproduction silk hangings for the ballroom were so perfect that when they were up even she couldn't spot the difference; and Jaz's third years were all thoroughly enjoying the preparations for the ball supper.

And today, on the day of the ball, it was snowing. Not enough to cause problems, but a light dusting—enough to make the house look really, really pretty.

Victoria loved the house in the snow. For her, Chiverton glowed brighter than any diamond.

Her professional life was perfect, right now. The house was looking better than ever. The fundraising week had put everyone on a real high. Today ought to be one of the happiest days of her life.

Except it wasn't.

She really, really missed Samuel. So did Humphrey; he looked up hopefully every time someone walked down the corridor to her office, and every time it wasn't Samuel he put his head back dejectedly between his paws. Right now, that was what Victoria wanted to do, too. Curl up in a ball and huddle in misery.

But tonight was the high point of the fund-raising week. She was expecting guests and the press any second now, and she needed to pin that smile on her face and be dazzling.

It was a week since his father's stroke. In that time Sam had done a lot of thinking. A lot of talking. A bit of persuading.

Tonight, he was hoping that the whole lot would come together. That he could fix the mess he'd made. His mother had given him wise advice; the Hamiltons had been shocked at first when he'd told them the truth about the 'engagement', but then they'd been understanding. Given him their blessing.

And now it was time to face Victoria.

He'd waited until the press had gone and the ball was in full swing. Just before supper, by his reckoning.

'Sam! I didn't think you were coming,' Jenny, the house steward stationed in the reception area, said. 'How's your dad?'

Obviously Victoria had explained his absence to everyone in terms of his father's illness, rather than pointing out that he'd let everyone down. 'He's on the mend, thanks.' He smiled at her. 'Everyone's upstairs?'

'They are. And you don't need anyone to show you the way to the ballroom, do you?'

'No. It's fine. But thanks.'

He strode up the massive curved staircase and through the Long Gallery. He could hear the music playing, and he looked through the doorway into the ballroom.

He'd seen the pictures on the website, but it hadn't prepared him for the real thing. Instead of that bare wall that made Victoria flinch, the silk hangings were back. The mirrors on the walls reflected the chandeliers, candelabra and each other, spreading the light further. And the walls actually glowed in the light.

It was stunning.

No wonder she loved this room.

The carpet had been removed temporarily; people were on the dance floor, following Michael the dancing master's instructions, and others were sitting on the *chaises longues* and chairs at the side of the room, watching them.

Victoria was dancing. In her red silk dress, she looked amazing, and his heart skipped a beat.

Please let her talk to him. Let her give him a chance.

He waited until the music had finished, then walked over to her. 'Good evening, Miss Hamilton.'

She stared at him, looking shocked. 'I thought you weren't coming tonight.'

'The night when the ballroom was back to its

former glory? Wild horses wouldn't have kept me away.' Though it wasn't the room he wanted. It was her.

'Is your dad all right?' she asked.

'He's home and grumbling at my mum about not being allowed a bacon sandwich. He's got all his words back, and the physio's having to tell him not to overdo things because he's so determined he wants to be back in the swing of things. Though he's agreed to let me take over the business.'

'Is that what you want?'

'It's part of what I want.' He looked at her. 'And that's why I'm here.'

She looked him up and down. 'But—your boots!'

'I know, I know, Regency men aren't supposed to wear boots to a ball. Mrs P told me. My dancing shoes are in a bag. I can't wear them outside or they'll be ruined—especially in the snow.' He smiled at her. 'Come with me?'

She shook her head. 'I can't. It's the middle of the ball.'

'Which looks as if it's going like clockwork. Jaz and the students have the food covered, Michael and the quartet have the dancing covered, and your dad will do whatever needs to be done.'

Her eyes narrowed at him. 'How do you know that?'

'Because I've spoken to your dad.'

Her frown deepened. 'He didn't tell me.'

Because Sam had asked him not to tell.

'What did you talk about?' she asked.

'By and by,' he said. 'Come with me, Victoria. Please.'

'Outside, you mean?' She frowned. 'But I'm…' She gestured to her dress.

'That's OK—I have an anachronistic blanket.' He smiled at her. 'I was going to get you a coat, but Mrs P said even she can't make a Regency woman's coat in an afternoon.'

'Pelisse,' she corrected.

He grinned, loving the fact she was being pernickety. 'And she also said that traditionally it was trimmed with fur, and I thought you might have a problem with that.'

'I do.'

'Hence the anachronistic blanket. It's downstairs by the front door.'

She gave in and let him shepherd her downstairs, where he wrapped the blanket round her.

'I need to get some shoes.'

'No, you don't.' He swept her up into his arms.

'Samuel! You can't—'

'Yes, I can,' he said, and marched her out of the house to the waiting carriage.

'Oh, my God,' she said, seeing the horses and carriage.

He grinned. 'To me they look white, but I've been told this is a pair of matched greys. I don't care if the carriage is anachronistic, I don't want you being frozen, and an open-topped carriage on a December night in England is impossible.' He deposited her in the carriage, made sure she was settled, and then sat opposite her.

'I…' She shook her head, as if unable to think of what to say.

He grinned. 'I've got you lost for words. That's good. This is my chance to talk.' He took a deep breath. 'First off, I owe you a huge apology.'

She looked at him, her dark eyes wide.

'When Dad had his stroke, I was really unfair to you. I pushed you away—even though I know I can trust you and you're not like Olivia. I didn't know how ill Dad would get, or if he'd die, and I didn't want to put you through that. And that's why I went all cold on you and basically—' He raked a hand through his hair. 'Yeah. Stupid, I should've talked to you and told you how I feel, but I'm a bloke and I'm not very good at that sort of thing.'

'Right. So you've kidnapped me in the middle of the fundraiser ball to tell me that.'

'No, I've kidnapped you for another reason,' he said. 'By and by. Firstly, I overheard what you said to Dad in the hospital.'

'Eavesdroppers,' she said primly, 'never hear any good about themselves.'

'Oh, but I did,' he said. 'That I would make an excellent job of anything I decided to do. Which is why—' He gestured round them. 'Technically, we don't need the suits and trappings. But I thought they'd be nice today. On a day when you've taken the house back two hundred years, it seemed appropriate to take my transport back two hundred years.'

'Only you would turn up in a landau with a pair of matched greys.'

He laughed. 'Trust you to know what the carriage is.'

She simply raised her eyebrows at him.

'Victoria. The reason I brought you out here is because I want to tell you that I love you. I've never felt like this about anyone. On paper, this shouldn't work. You're this massive history nerd and I work with figures. You live in the middle of nowhere with your parents and my house is a total bachelor pad in a very trendy bit of London.' He took a deep breath. 'But.'

'But?'

'It's you,' he said. 'Everything about you. I love that you're so serious and you pay attention to detail. I love that you pour your heart and soul into what you do. I love that you're the centre of your family—your parents adore you and your dog adores you and everyone who works in the house just lights up when you walk by because you pay attention and you listen to them and they know it.' He reached over to her and took her hand. 'But most of all I love you for you.'

'Uh-huh.'

'Which is Victoria-speak for the fact you don't know what to say.' He removed the glove from her left hand. 'I have actually done this the right way, this time. I talked to your parents about our fake engagement.'

'You did what?' She looked horrified.

'Actually, they understood. But we need to stop with the fake engagement business.'

'Agreed.'

'And the reason we need to stop with the fake one,' he said, 'is because I want it to be a real one. Let's be clear: it's *you* I want, not the house.'

'So you don't want to live here?'

'I want to live with you, whether it's here or in a—' He cast about for the most unlikely thing he could think of. 'In a yurt.'

She laughed, then. 'A yurt?'

'A yurt pitched in the middle of a swamp,' he said. 'I don't care where I live, as long as it's with you. And that's why I talked to your parents. Asking permission and stuff.' He dropped to one knee and took a velvet-covered box from his pocket. 'So this is why I kidnapped you from the ball. I love you—and, even though I haven't given you the chance to say it, I think you feel the same way about me, or you wouldn't have woken up in my arms that morning and you wouldn't have said what you did to Dad. And if Dad hadn't had that stroke, we would still have been having this conversation. Maybe not in the middle of the ball and maybe not in a carriage in the snow, but we would still definitely have been having this conversation. I've wanted to have this conversation with you for weeks.' He took a deep breath and opened the box. 'Will you marry me, Victoria?'

The ring nestled among the velvet was very simple, a single diamond set in platinum, and Victoria loved it.

And she loved the effort he'd put into this, too. That he'd clearly visited Mrs Prinks to get the right kind of boots, that he'd hired a carriage and horses, that he knew her tastes well enough to buy the perfect engagement ring—and he'd asked her parents, too, so he had their blessing before he proposed and obviously her mother had told him her ring size.

But most of all he'd said the important things. That he loved her. Loved her for *herself.* Loved the things about her that her exes had all found annoying.

She swallowed hard. Time for her to say it. And it was different, saying it when you knew the other person felt the same way. 'I love you, too, Sammy.'

He blinked. 'Did you just call me Sammy?'

She nodded. 'And I guess you can…call me Tori.' The pet name he'd wanted to call her before, but she'd refused.

He kissed her and slid the ring onto her finger. 'I love you, Tori,' he said softly. 'And now we're going back to the ball before you freeze. How the hell did they do all this stuff in Regency times?'

'You must be freezing, too, in that frock coat.'

'Come and dance with me and we'll warm up,' he said. 'You were supposed to keep a waltz free for me.'

'I would've done, but you weren't there when they played the waltz.'

He laughed and kissed her again. 'Michael will get them to play another one for us. Especially as I have champagne on ice.'

She frowned. 'How did you manage that?'

'I had it delivered to your dad.'

'What if I'd said no?' she asked, suddenly curious.

'Then I would've written you really bad poetry and worn you down until you agreed.'

'Bad poetry.' She grinned. 'If I'd known that,

I might've said no. Just to see how bad your poetry is.'

'Too late. You're wearing my ring now.' He drew her hand up to his mouth and kissed the inside of her wrist. 'Seriously, if you'd said no, then I asked your dad to give everyone champagne on my behalf to celebrate the ballroom restoration. And then I would've found myself a yurt and started writing bad poetry.' He raised an eyebrow. 'Actually, as you seem interested, I might do the poetry anyway. And I'll grow my hair out like Byron's. Be "mad and bad and dangerous to know".'

'Oh, please,' she said, laughing.

'Wait, wait. I have good, proper Regency poetry. Which I admit Jude found for me.' He coughed. '"She walks in beauty, like the night…" And you do. I love you.' He kissed her again. 'And you've just made me the happiest person in the world. Thank you.'

She felt her eyes fill with tears. 'I love you, too, Sammy.'

He carried her back to the house, then changed his boots for the dancing shoes.

'I can't believe you bought Regency boots just for tonight,' she said as they walked up the staircase together.

'Oh, I have plans for those boots.' He raised an eyebrow. 'They're the perfect footwear for whenever I want to carry my wife off some-where and play Darcy to her Miss Bennet.'

She laughed.

'But keep your hands behind your back for now,' he said. 'Our parents need to be the first to know.'

Back in the ballroom, they went over to her parents. 'Can I borrow you both for a quick word?' Samuel asked.

Patrick and Diana looked thrilled and led them out to the Long Gallery.

'Anachronistic but necessary,' he said, taking his phone from his pocket. 'Excuse me a second. My parents need to be in this conversation as well.' He put the phone on speaker, waited while the line connected, and the call was picked up within two rings.

'Sammy?' Denise asked. 'What did she say?'

Her parents looked as if they were desperate to know the answer, too.

Victoria brought her hands from behind her back to show the engagement ring and smiled. 'I said yes.'

EPILOGUE

A year later

PATRICK STOOD BY the piano and the string quartet. 'I'm delighted to welcome you all to the second annual Chiverton Christmas ball—a tradition started by my wonderful daughter Victoria. And it's time for our first dance.'

'Well, the Hon Mrs Hamilton-Weatherby, it's all looking very festive. And oh, look, we're under the kissing ball.' Samuel stole a kiss. 'I still think we should have tinsel.'

Victoria knew he was teasing her. 'Not on your life.'

'Anachronistic,' he said with a grin. 'Come and waltz with me.'

They were in the middle of the ballroom when she said to him, 'The thing about Regency waltzes is that you were close enough to whisper secrets.'

'Oh, yes?'

'I would say that I love you, but that's not a secret.'

He laughed. 'I love it when your eyes are full of mischief. So what are you going to tell me, then?'

Demurely, she turned in a circle with him. 'Our honeymoon.' He'd taken her on a mini version of the Grand Tour, and she'd loved every second of it, sharing the museums and art galleries with him. He'd even talked the orchestra outside Florian's in Venice into playing a Regency waltz so he could dance with her through St Mark's Square.

'What about it?'

'It seems,' she said, 'it had consequences.'

'Consequences?'

'That's the thing about Regency dress,' she said, enjoying herself. 'The Empire neckline is very flattering. It hides bumps.'

'Bumps?' He sucked in a breath. 'Are you telling me we're…?'

She nodded. 'Two months. I thought I just missed a period because we were so busy. But I did a test this morning. I've been waiting for the right moment to tell you.'

'I didn't think I could be any happier, but…' He beamed at her. 'That's amazing. I really hope you're ready for this baby to be utterly spoiled by two sets of grandparents.'

'Not to mention the baby's doting papa,' she said with a smile.

'If it's a girl,' he said softly, 'maybe we can call her Lizzie.'

'I'd like that.'

'Just think,' he said. 'Last year the ball was our engagement. This year, it's our news. Next year…'

She grinned. 'Next year I'm sure the Weatherby Wonder will think of something.'

He laughed back. 'Just you wait…'

* * * * *

*If you enjoyed this story,
check out these other great reads
from Kate Hardy*

Reunited at the Altar
Christmas Bride for the Boss
The Runaway Bride and the Billionaire
His Shy Cinderella

All available now!